When nothing goes right...

I had beaten Keith. Big deal. He was likely high on something and I had taken advantage of it. Beating him didn't change the fact that Marietta had dumped me. I was still going to have to put on an act so everybody would think I didn't care. I was sick of it! Always trying to put on an act. But what else could I do? I couldn't let anyone know how I really felt inside. They'd all laugh at me. After all, I was Shane Donahue; I was supposed to be tough; or so I'd wanted everyone to think.

I reached the street and kept moving, one foot in front of another. Stupid thoughts raced through my mind. What would happen if a car should come racing along and skid on the ice and run over me? Would this pain deep inside go away?

As if on command, the headlights of a car appeared, coming straight toward me, shining on the falling snowflakes so that they looked like enormous white feathers floating down from a gigantic cloud pillow fight in the sky.

Books by N. J. Lindquist

Novels for teens

"Circle of Friends" series
Best of Friends
Friends Like These

"Growing Up, Taking Hold" series
In Time of Trouble

Non-fiction for teens
The Bridge—Part 1
The Bridge—Part 2

Adult Mystery
Shaded Light: A Manziuk/Ryan Mystery

http://members.homo.net/thats-life

Growing Up, Taking Hold...

IN TIME OF TROUBLE

N. J. Lindquist

That's Life! Communications

Markham, Canada

In Time of Trouble

That's Life! Communications
Box 487, Markham, ON L3P 3R1
Call tollfree 1-877-THATSLI(FE)
Email: thats-life@home.com
http://members.home.net/thats-life

Cover design: John Gruchy

Canadian Cataloguing in Publication Data

Lindquist, N. J. (Nancy J.), 1948-
  In time of trouble

ISBN: 0-9685495-0-0

I. In Time of Trouble.

PS8573.I5317515 1999   jC813'.54   C99-931478-5
PZ7.L65925In 1999

To the main guys in my life:
Les, Kit, Mark, Daniel, and Jeffrey

1

"Shane, you're late." Mr. Kaufmann was standing in the office doorway when I walked into the warehouse Friday after school. He had his hands on his hips, and it didn't take a genius to know he wasn't happy.

"Yeah, I know I'm late. But—"

He turned his back on my explanation and walked into the office.

I started to follow, but he returned almost immediately.

"I was going to wait until tomorrow," he said, "but there's no point. Here's the money we owe you. You're fired."

He held out an envelope, but I didn't take it.

"I said you're fired," Mr. Kaufmann repeated. "The only reason I've kept you on this long is that you worked well last summer when you were here full time. But since school started and you've been part-time—well, it just hasn't worked out."

"I don't get it. You're firing me because I was late today? I can explain that."

"It isn't today. It's your attitude. You do the least you can get away with. You really don't care if you do a good job or not. And some of the new kids are copying you. I can't have that. So here's your money."

He held the envelope in front of my face and this time I took it. But I felt more like stuffing it down his throat. What was to care about in moving boxes and loading trucks? I'd been doing the job, hadn't I? Spending every day after school and all day Saturday in this stinking place!

He went into the office and shut the door, so there was nothing for me to do but leave.

I knew the others were watching. Well, I didn't owe them anything. They were no friends of mine—just people I worked with.

I swore under my breath and walked back the way I'd come, grabbing my jacket off the hook as I went by.

And then I noticed the small tear on the sleeve.

How had that happened? Last night when I'd put my car in the shed and had brushed against the wall? I'd bought the jacket, an expensive black leather one, in the after-Christmas sale only a couple of weeks ago. Because of all the repairs to my car, and other expenses, the jacket had taken the last of my money. Now the jacket was already torn and the pay packet I was holding contained all the money I had left after working my butt off all summer and fall!

Anger surged through me. There was a stack of boxes near the doorway. I kicked them over, feeling a small amount of satisfaction when one of them opened and a bunch of small ball bearings went rolling all over the floor. I yanked open the side door and slammed it behind me as hard as I could.

The January cold cooled me off fast. I stopped to put on the jacket.

This was all my dad's fault! Just because I'd had another speeding ticket, he'd taken the keys to my car and told me I couldn't have them back for two weeks. And because I'd had to walk to work, I was late. So I was out of a job and it was all his fault.

I decided to go over to Ted's apartment and see if he was alone. Ted and I had been hanging around together a lot since last summer. He's a bit like me—eighteen and tired of being treated like a little kid. But we look kind of funny together. I'm blond, six-two, fairly muscular, and, they say, good-looking. Ted's short, maybe five-seven, and skinny—about a hundred and thirty pounds dripping wet. He has long, brown hair and a thin face with sharp features. Not exactly the guy you'd introduce to your favorite sister.

Our backgrounds are different, too. I've got a dad who's worked for the same company since he was my age, a mom who works part-time at the library, and a twin brother, Sandy. Ted lives in an apartment with only his father, who's had a ton of jobs and right now is a salesman for a men's clothing manufacturer. That means he travels a lot, which means Ted gets left alone a lot, which he likes.

Ted's kind of strange. His marks in school are terrible, but his street smarts would put him at the top of the class. He thinks life should be one big party, but, despite his size, he can defend himself pretty well when he has to.

His apartment is on the top floor of a four-story building. It's nothing to write home about, but it serves its purpose. Neither Ted nor his dad are what you'd call fussy.

When I got up to his door, I knocked, and I heard him yell, "Who is it?"

"Shane."

I heard him pulling back bolts. Then the door opened.

"Your dad here?" I asked.

"Naw, it's okay. I thought you worked today."

"No."

"Must have heard wrong."

Time enough to enlighten him later.

We spent several hours watching a movie he'd borrowed and drinking a few beers. Then we sent out for pizza. Stupid on my part because I should have saved what money I had left. Also stupid because if I didn't go home for supper my dad would be mad.

But sometimes it's easier not to face things. And this was one of those times.

So we ate pizza, had a couple more beers, and watched TV until suddenly Ted commented that it was eight o'clock.

Reality intruded. I jumped. "I'm supposed to pick up Marietta!"

"How?"

I stared at him. "What do you mean—how?" Then I remembered I had no car. And I hadn't arranged for a ride. I sat down.

"Get a ride with somebody."

"Yeah." I phoned a couple of kids and finally got some-body who'd pick me up and drive me to Marietta's. Ted came, too.

There was a party at Scott's house. Scott is another friend—well, sort of a friend. His parents are away a lot, so Scott has parties at his house frequently. I don't know if his parents are so stupid they can't tell, or if they just don't care.

Anyway, they never get in his way, so he keeps on having parties.

And that's where I was taking Marietta, the girl I had been going out with since last September. She's really something. Hard to believe she'd actually been going with me that long. That's a lot longer than she usually gives one guy.

She wasn't too pleased when she came to the door of her house. "You're late." She sounded a lot like Mr. Kaufmann.

"Sorry."

"Where's your car?"

"I told you my dad took my keys."

"You mean you really can't drive it?"

"I told you this morning."

"Well, I guess I didn't quite believe it."

"Now do you?"

She handed me her long, white, furry coat and I sort of held it for her to get her arms in. I'm not very good at things like that, but she got it on in spite of my help, and soon we were in the back seat of the car.

I pulled her closer, but she pushed me away.

"You've been drinking," she said.

"So?"

"So nothing. I wanted to talk to you."

"What about?"

"Are you sober enough to listen?"

"I only had a couple of drinks."

"I don't want to talk here."

"Neither do I." I pulled her close again, and this time she let me kiss her a couple of times. But she wasn't into it.

We arrived at Scott's, but instead of going in, Marietta walked around to the side of the house. She stepped carefully, keeping to the dried brown grass and avoiding the patches of snow and mud. I figured this must really be important for her to walk on the lawn in her stiletto heels, so I followed.

"So, what do you want to talk about?"

"I think it's time," she said.

"Time?"

"We've been going together nearly four months."

"So?"

"You were a lot of fun."

"Were?"

"That's right. Were. You aren't any more. In fact, lately you're boring."

"So you're tired of me? And that's it? Just like that?"

She elaborated on the subject, but I barely heard. I felt a bit like I was watching a show on TV. Like I wasn't really part of it. All I could concentrate on was Marietta herself, and not what she was saying. Her silky, blond hair, which fell loose to just below her waist, shimmered as she spoke. One of those crazy three-inch-high heels she wears lifted and stamped impatiently now and again. Even with those heels, she's so tiny the top of her head barely comes to my shoulder. And the figure under that coat! Marietta wears halter tops and short tight skirts and looks the way most girls just dream about.

But I couldn't see her figure right now. All I could see were her hands, punctuated with blue nail polish, moving rapidly to emphasize the words she was saying. And her animated face, with its black lashes, blue shadows, and red lipstick, looking up earnestly, innocently, at me, as if I should understand and be happy to do this for her.

As I watched her, I realized how little she cared about me. Shane Donahue was just one more in a long line of admirers. She'd given me all her attention for several months. But I was no longer entertaining her. And I had no car. So it was time.

I stood there, leaning against the wall, waiting for her explanation to end. I don't know how I should have felt. Angry, sad, whatever....All I really felt was numb. Added to the rest, what difference did it make whether Marietta dumped me or not? It was just another pebble to add to the pile of things that hadn't worked out for Shane Donahue. That pile was getting pretty high.

Through the mist I heard Keith's name, and something triggered my tongue.

"Keith?" I echoed.

"Yes. Do you have a problem with that?"

"You're going to go out with him?"

"Why not? I probably should have long ago."

Yeah. It made sense.

Why not Marietta and Keith? Why should the fact that Keith and I had been good friends since last summer mean Keith would stop at stealing my girl?

"Are you angry?" she asked.

I brushed strands of hair back from my face while I thought about it. Was I angry?

"Where's Keith?" I asked after a moment.

She shrugged. "In the house, I expect."

I remembered the first time I'd gotten up enough nerve to ask Marietta out. She'd been going with Rory Jefferson at the time, and she said no. I asked her again a week later, and this time she said yes. But Rory objected and I ended up fighting him. Keith had been there, impartial since Rory was a friend of his, too. But when I won, Keith slapped me on the back and laughed and told me I deserved her. Was I supposed to fight for her now? And if I won, would I get her back? Was that all she really wanted? Guys fighting over her?

I don't know what she was expecting. I guess she thought I'd make some effort to make her change her mind.

But I didn't.

I walked away without a word. When I looked back, she was staring after me, her mouth open.

I found Keith sitting at the kitchen table by himself drinking beer and looking at a magazine. And waiting.

Keith is sort of a big shot. Not at school, where he's short on ambition, and not with the "in" crowd, like Sandy, but with kids like Ted and me.

Keith is big, a little taller than me and at least forty pounds heavier. But he's not fat. In fact, he's put together like an armored tank. Like Ted, he's always willing to party, but if he had a choice he'd take a good fight. And he usually wins. He looks the part too, with partly shaved black hair, swarthy skin, and a large nose that was broken once and never put quite straight again.

I stood in front of him, waiting, and at last he looked up. "Well?" he challenged.

"Thanks, pal," I said evenly.

"All's fair in love and war," Keith retorted. "You'd do the same to me."

"Maybe."

He pushed his chair back. "So? Are you going to be reasonable or do I have to fight you?"

I considered. I'd never fought Keith. Was I afraid to? Maybe, but I didn't think so. More important, did I want to fight him? To give Marietta the satisfaction of seeing us down on the floor kicking and gouging each other because of her? And what difference would it make, anyway? Even if I won, did I want her that way?

"Well, Blondie?" Keith used a nickname he knows I hate. He was grinning, and I knew he'd love to fight me just for the excitement of it.

The anger that had been building up inside me all day took over. Yeah, that's what I wanted, too. I'd feel a lot better after a good fight.

Ted came into the kitchen. "What you two doing? Where's Marietta, Shane."

I ignored him.

"What you up to? Trying something new?" Ted asked, grabbing my sleeve.

"Well?" Keith repeated.

I unbuttoned my jacket.

"What are you doing?" Ted asked for a third time, now getting impatient. "You spaced out? Try something you didn't like?"

I shook my head and handed him my jacket. "Here, take this and get out of the kitchen."

He took the jacket, but continued to question me. "What are—"

As I let go of the jacket, Keith's fist struck my jaw and only the presence of the kitchen table kept me from going down. Keith stood in front of me grinning. I came up slowly, watching him. For all his size, he was like a cat, and I knew I had to watch for my opportunity.

"Come on, Blondie. What'cha waiting for? Scared?"

The doorway was crowded with kids. Ted and Marietta and others. All of them calling out, egging us on, anxious for the fight to continue.

Keith glanced sideways and I let go a right that should have done some damage. But he had been toying with me, and my

13

fist glanced off his cheek as he dodged to the left and sent a fist into my stomach. Again, I was off-balance, and he followed up with a left to my chin. I knew I had to forget about the anger I was feeling, and concentrate on what I was doing.

Keith was enjoying himself. "Hey, Blondie, I thought you could fight. That's what I've heard, anyway."

"Come on, Shane, you've got him," someone urged.

"You can take him easily, Keith." Marietta's voice.

"Two to one on Keith," Scott yelled. "Any takers?"

I blocked out the voices as I began moving sideways, pushing a chair out of the way, moving around Keith the way a boxer does his opponent in the ring, looking for an opening in his defense. I was focused now. First Keith. Then everything else.

He had his fists up like a boxer would, protecting his face. The last thing he expected was for me to charge in, grab him around the waist, and drag him to the ground. So that's what I did. Hey, nobody laid out any rules, did they? I tackled him hard, and I heard a big, "Oof!" as we went down hard onto the beige linoleum, me on top.

He grabbed my hair and I gave him what in boxing would have been called a low blow and disallowed. But we had no referee. While he was yelling in pain, I followed up with a right to the nose that brought blood gushing out. He yelled and pulled my hair and tried to get a thumb in my eye, but I moved away and got to my feet. Warily, he started to get up. I waited till he was half-way, then tackled him again, throwing him to his stomach and grabbing his leg. I twisted it up behind and he yelled and swore

"Give up?" I asked.

He swore at me, and tried to grab my leg, but I tightened my grip on his ankle until he stopped.

I had always suspected I could beat Keith. Okay, maybe not if we had a referee and rules and all. But in a situation like this, when you could do anything, I'd always seemed to have advantage. Maybe it was because I didn't care what I did so long as I won.

"I win?" I asked.

Keith nodded. His face was red and he looked as if he were in some pain.

"I didn't hear you," I said.

"You win." His words were slurred. Probably because his nose was still spilling blood all over. If it was broken, as I thought it might well be, I hoped they set it straight this time.

"Marietta?" I asked.

"You—you can keep her."

"That right, Marietta?" I turned to where she was standing in the doorway.

"You beat him," was all she said.

"Yeah, but does that mean I get to keep you?"

She shrugged. "I guess."

"Come here."

Reluctantly, she pushed past Ted and Scott and came to within a foot of me. She had taken off her coat, so I could see that terrific figure.

I let go of Keith's leg, and he collapsed on the floor, moaning. Scott went rushing to get a towel to stop the blood from getting all over the floor. "Idiots," he said cheerfully.

"Way to go, Shane!" Ted yelled. Several other people called out congratulations to me or sympathy to Keith.

I put my arm around Marietta's tiny waist. "So what happens now?" I asked.

She reached up to put her arm around my neck and started to kiss me, but I put my hand over her lips.

"What's wrong?"

"I changed my mind."

2

Marietta stared up at me. "What are you talking about?"

"It isn't worth it."

"What are you talking about?"

"You. You aren't worth fighting for. Hey, Keith! I changed my mind. She's all yours."

I pushed Marietta toward Keith and turned to shove my way through the crowd that was still crushed into the doorway.

But Marietta wasn't about to let me go.

She grabbed my shirt and yelled, "You pig!"

I turned to face her and her nails raked the side of my neck.

I slapped her hard across the face. She staggered back, swearing at me.

"Somebody told me you had no class," I said. "I hit him for saying it, but I guess he was right after all. My sympathies, Keith."

I turned and pushed through the crowd. A couple of girls asked me to come dance with them, but I didn't stop.

It was only when I got to the door that I remembered my jacket. When I yelled, Ted came running to give it to me.

"Wow, you really hammered him," Ted said.

"Yeah."

Maybe I should have felt good about it, but for some reason I didn't. Maybe because of Marietta.

"You going?"

"Yeah."

"Want me to come?"

"No. You stay. Have a good time. I'll see you tomorrow."

"You sure you're okay? I could come if you want."

"Tomorrow," I repeated more firmly. Then I walked quickly away in the direction of my house.

I slowed down after a few blocks.

The adrenaline that had come surging up when I faced Keith had seeped away, and I felt sick to my stomach. Ahead of me was a small children's park. In the cold darkness, the swings hung lifelessly and the slide and jungle gym stood empty. They looked lonely and deserted, just the way I felt.

My feet turned in. Walking over to the wooden jungle gym, I grasped two of the poles, spread out my feet, and leaned my head against the hard wood. My whole body was heaving. I heard sobs, and felt wetness on my cheeks. For maybe five minutes, I just stood there, crying like I was a little lost kid. Finally, I got control again and wiped my face with the sleeve of my jacket. I remembered the rip in it and wondered if it could be fixed.

Suddenly, I realized someone might have seen me. I hurriedly looked around. But only the dark images of the playground stared back. I was all alone.

I sat on one of the swings—something I hadn't done for years. Idly, I moved the swing back and forth. Funny. Things were so easy when you were a kid. They didn't really prepare you for now, when you were nearly grown up and life seemed to take one punch after another, not even giving you time to get set in between. This past year, everything had gone wrong. Like somebody changed all the rules without bothering to tell me. Or maybe it was me. Maybe I had changed. After all, Sandy seemed to be doing okay.

My eyes blurred and I shoved my feet against the sand so the swing moved crazily. Why did I always wind up thinking about my twin?

I stopped the swing and stood up. I kicked viciously at the sand, but all I did was get some of it in my shoe.

After I'd put the shoe back on and put my collar up so no one would see the scratches, I started walking. It was beginning to snow—large flakes that glided softly from the heavens and melted where they lay.

But I barely noticed the snowflakes. I had beaten Keith. Big deal. He was likely high on something and I had taken advantage of it. Beating him didn't change the fact that Marietta had dumped me. I was still going to have to put on an act so everybody would think I didn't care. I was sick of it! Always trying to put on an act. But what else could I do? I couldn't let anyone

17

know how I really felt inside. They'd all laugh at me. After all, I was Shane Donahue; I was supposed to be tough; or so I'd wanted everyone to think.

I reached the street and kept moving, one foot in front of another. Stupid thoughts raced through my mind. What would happen if a car should come racing along and skid on the ice and run over me? Would this pain deep inside go away?

As if on command, the headlights of a car appeared, coming straight toward me, shining on the falling snowflakes so that they looked like enormous white feathers floating down from a gigantic cloud pillow fight in the sky.

The car, an old, blue station wagon, was going slowly and it didn't skid. Instead, the driver slowed to a stop and a head appeared out of the window.

A female voice said, "Need a lift?"

I stared through the darkness, trying to make out her identity. Short, dark brown hair, an expressive face....

"Do you want a ride?" she asked again, and this time I placed her. Janice Hopkins. I knew her name, but she was two years below me in school, and she wasn't one of Sandy's or my friends.

But what the heck?

I moved toward the car, and she said, "It *is* Shane, isn't it?" Her voice was soft and musical.

"Yeah."

"You look cold."

I shrugged.

"Do you need a ride? I mean, you seem to be walking and.... Well, I've got my dad's car tonight, so if you need a ride, I know where you live."

I got in. As we started moving, I sat wondering what to say. I wasn't exactly in a talkative mood. Still, I had to say something. "Your dad let you have the car much?"

"I just got my license two weeks ago. You have your own car, don't you?"

"More or less."

"What?"

"I have a car, but I've had three speeding tickets, so I can't drive it for two weeks. My father's idea. You had a ticket yet?"

She shook her head.

"I wouldn't mind getting them if my parents didn't find out. They think it's some big deal."

"Don't you lose your license if you get too many?"

"Yeah, I guess."

We lapsed into silence again.

"You're in Weaver's class, aren't you?" I asked after a while. "Home room, I mean."

"Yes."

"He's weird, huh? I had him two years ago."

Her eyes were focused straight ahead as she concentrated on driving. "He's okay."

I gazed at her in disbelief. Anyone who thought Weaver was okay had to be a little strange herself!

She glanced over and laughed. Her laugh was carefree and melodic, and I remembered hearing it in the hallways and wondering what she was like.

"Okay, he is a bit weird," she conceded. "But he's a good teacher if you ignore his eccentricities."

"If you say so."

Her eyes twinkled. Then she was watching the road again, stopping for a red light, and driving very carefully.

We were close to my house, so I gave directions and Janice stopped in front. "Well, thanks for the ride." I got out and started toward the house. Then I thought about facing my parents and changed my mind. I stopped dead.

"Shane?" She hadn't driven away.

I turned back towards the car, walked around to her side and opened the door. "I've got a better idea. Let's go someplace."

Janice batted her lashes and smiled. "Sure, why not?"

"Move over and let me drive. The roads are getting slippery."

"Oh, come on. Your dad won't let you drive your car, so I should let you drive mine? What if you got a speeding ticket? Then my dad would have a fit. Besides, he told me not to let anyone else drive."

I swore. Then I tried again, "So what? You don't have to tell him."

"But if he found out, he might never let me have the car again. And, anyway, why should you drive instead of me? I'm safe." She glanced up at me from under those long lashes and said provocatively, "What's the matter? Don't you think I can drive?"

Embarrassed, I scuffed the road with the toe of my running shoe. "Naw, it's not that."

"Don't you like to have a girl drive you?"

I grinned guiltily.

"Chauvinist."

I stood holding the door open.

"Chicken," she said.

I shut the door and walked around to the passenger side. After a second, I got in.

"Are you going to open the doors for me, too?" I asked.

"Not on your life."

"I take it that means you won't pay, either?"

She looked at me sideways and then smiled. "Not unless I have to. I'm not crazy about doing dishes."

I laughed. I felt good for the first time today. Maybe things weren't so bad after all.

I directed her to the parking lot at a nearby McDonald's and laughed again at the way she maneuvered the car. Then I got out and opened the door for her. As she stepped out, she reached down, scooped up a handful of snow, and jumped up to shove it down the back of my neck.

"Hey, what was that for?"

"For being a rotten back seat driver."

"Tough girl, huh?"

"I've got three brothers."

"Lucky you. One's enough for me. More than enough!"

She gave me a funny look, but didn't ask any questions.

"Come on, I'm starved." I grabbed her hand. "You hungry?"

"Not really."

"I am."

We found a table in a corner and I ordered a hamburger and two milkshakes. I ate slowly, talking about school and teachers and people we both knew. She noticed the top of the scratches and asked. I just said I had scratched myself on a fence. She gave me a funny look, but didn't say anything more. Just kept playing with her straw, barely touching her milkshake. I finally finished it for her. Then I stretched. "Well, are you ready to take me home?"

Janice laughed. "That doesn't sound quite right, does it?"

"Well, if you think I'm going to go with you to your place and then walk home, you're crazy. Tell you what, you can phone me when you get there. That way I'll know you're okay."

We walked slowly back to the car. Janice had the keys in her hand, so I took them and opened the door to the driver's side. But I stood in her way. "You still want to drive?"

She smiled. "If you didn't get speeding tickets you'd be driving your own car."

"If I'd been driving my own car, I might not have met you."

She laughed. "Maybe I'd have made you meet me."

"Oh, really? What would you have done? Asked me out?"

"You'll never know."

I leaned forward to take her hand and she didn't draw back. Then I looked into her eyes for a second. There was no sign of unwillingness, so I kissed her cheek. She turned her face up and I kissed her. Then I moved out of the way. "Okay, you drive. Here are the keys."

I kept my arm on the back of the seat so I could gently touch her hair and neck. She didn't seem to mind. She drove carefully to my house. When she stopped, I reached over and shut off the motor. "You aren't in a hurry, are you?"

"That depends. I don't want you to think I'm too easy."

I laughed and pulled her closer.

After a while, she said, "What time is it?"

"It's too dark to see."

She turned the light on.

I looked at my watch. "A quarter to twelve."

"I had no idea it was that late. I have to be in by twelve."

"Time flies when you're having fun."

She looked up at me intently. "Are you?"

"Am I what?"

"Having fun."

"You mean do I like being with you?"

She nodded.

"Stupid. Don't you know when a guy likes you?"

"I wasn't wondering about 'a guy.' I was wondering about you."

"Well, maybe this will answer your question." I slipped my arms around to hold her. Then I really kissed her.

After she had caught her breath, she said, "I bet you say that to all the girls."

"Nope. Only a select few."

"Does that mean I'll see you again?"

"Try to avoid me."

"Good-night."

"Good night, Janice. Call me when you get home."

I watched as the car drove away. Life felt a little better. In fact, I was humming as I walked toward the two-story semi-detached house where we'd lived for six years. Even having to look through all my pockets for the keys didn't bother me. I found them at last, and even remembered to put my jacket and shoes into the closet next to the front door instead of tossing them on the floor.

Mom and Dad were in bed, so I grabbed the phone before it finished ringing the first time, and talked to Janice just long enough for her to tell me she got home okay. After that, I went to the basement where we keep our computer.

I was looking around on the Internet when I heard Sandy unlock the front door. He must have noticed the light was on because a moment later he came downstairs. Seeing me, he jerked back in surprise.

"You home?"

"Yeah."

"How was your evening? You and Marietta have a good time?"

I felt a stab of pain in my guts, but I said, "Fine," and hoped he didn't know.

"Oh, come on," he said, "you haven't been home this early on a Friday night for the last year. You really think I'm going to believe everything's fine?"

"I don't care what you believe! Leave me alone."

"What's the matter? Too much to drink? Or maybe Marietta stabbed you with one of her nails and you lost so much blood you had to come home to bed to recover. Am I close?"

I shut off the computer. "I'm going to bed."

"Okay," said Sandy. "You don't have to tell me."

"That's right. I don't."

I headed upstairs, leaving him to turn off the lights.

I went into the bathroom and shut the door. But instead of brushing my teeth and getting ready for bed, I just leaned against the door, feeling sick. Every time Sandy and I were anywhere near each other these days, we seemed to fight.

But it hadn't always been that way. In fact, up until this past year we'd been pretty well inseparable. We'd spent hours together, building Lego space ships, playing catch, riding bikes, reading comic books huddled together in one bunk until Mom had made us separate to go to sleep.

We'd even had our own language when we were little. Not that we needed words. We'd always known when the other was sad or afraid or angry. And if anyone hurt one of us, the other would be out for revenge.

When we were eleven, we'd moved from our cramped apartment into this house where there were three bedrooms, and Dad had wanted to give us each his own room. Instead, we'd persuaded him to knock down the wall between so we could have one big room together.

But, somehow, this past year, we had drifted apart. Sandy had become popular, and last June had been elected school president. He was the fair-haired boy—everyone liked him—teachers, parents, kids—everyone!

And for some reason, I didn't fit in with his new friends. So I'd made my own. Only, somehow, it wasn't the same. And these past months, while everything in my life seemed to be falling apart, he was doing just fine.

I was failing a couple of classes; Sandy was getting straight A's. I had been kicked off the basketball team, which was the only team I'd made; Sandy was the star of several school teams. Just last night Dad had grounded my car because I'd had too many speeding tickets; Sandy never got speeding tickets. I had just been fired from my crummy job and because I had spent my money buying a car and insurance and gas, I was now broke; Sandy had had a high-paying, interesting job last summer where he'd been able to save enough money so he didn't have to work during the year. I had just been dumped by a girl Sandy said you couldn't pay him to date; he was dating the head cheerleader, who just happened to be the most popular girl in the school.

I shook my head. What use was it to think about him. We were like strangers now, and there wasn't a single thing I could do about it.

I got ready for bed and was under the covers when Sandy came up. I lay still, hearing him get ready for bed. Taking off his good slacks and his shirt. Putting on his pajamas. Combing his hair. Making sure he looked good, as usual. Funny, even though we're identical twins, anybody who knows us can tell us apart easily. For starters, his hair is shorter than mine, and styled, and he's always combing it to make sure it's in place. But more than that, he wears pants and shirts, and maybe a sweater, and looks like he's always trying to impress somebody. I prefer jeans and T-shirts. And I don't smile all the time, like he does. Or worry about things like aftershave. And hanging up clothes.

But at last he was ready for bed. He switched off the light. For about a minute, it was quiet. Then, "I heard something happened about your job today."

"I'm trying to get some sleep, if you don't mind."

I heard him moving in bed and then the light went back on.

"Yes, as a matter of fact, I do mind. You're my brother. And we used to be pretty good friends. But I don't seem to know you any more. It's almost as if my twin has gone away and someone else has taken his place. What's gone wrong?"

"Nothing's wrong."

"Don't lie to me."

"Oh, did you remember? I lie all the time. Well, my dear brother, nothing is wrong! I think you are just as perfect as ever—maybe more so, and I'm going to sleep."

"Shane, don't. Please. I don't understand you any more. We used to be best friends, and now—"

"And now I'm a lot smarter than I was then. What are you worried about, anyway? You've got everything you need. Or do you want me bowing and scraping along with everyone else?"

"Don't be ridiculous. I just don't want to feel my own brother hates me."

"I don't hate you."

"Well, you sure act as if you do."

I swore at him.

"Thanks."

"Look, you take care of your life and I'll take care of mine."

"From what I've seen lately, you're doing a lousy job."

I wanted to argue, but the truth was he was probably right. So should I tell him he was right and I was a creep, or should I use my fists to make him eat his words?

I did neither, and a wall of silence rose.

Sandy broke it at last by getting out of his bed and walking across to sit on the edge of mine. "Shane, I'm sorry. I shouldn't have said that. Shane, can't you see I'm just worried about you? If you keep on acting the way you have been, you're going to get expelled. I don't want that to happen. Shane?"

I hated him then. Because he could be so objective. Because he had no idea what it felt like to be me. Between clenched teeth, I yelled, "Go to hell!."

"Shane!"

3

I turned over and swung, catching Sandy by surprise. The force of my blow sent him tumbling off the bed onto the floor. But he was up immediately, and now his eyes flashed.

"Get out of that bed!"

"What's the matter? Can't you take it?"

"Get out before I drag you out!"

"I'd like to see you try."

Sandy, now furious, reached to grab my arm and pull me onto the floor. "Get up!"

"Make me!"

Sandy pulled on my arm, and we landed in a heap on the floor. He aimed a blow at my chin, but I saw it coming and ducked. The blow glanced off my shoulder, and I threw one of my own, but it didn't do any damage. Then Sandy caught me a good one on the mouth, and I fell hard against the bed, the taste of blood on my lips. Sandy got up, looking worried, like he wanted to quit, but I lunged head-first and gave him one in the stomach that made him take notice, and then we were in close, jabbing and pushing.

We were going at it, giving blow for blow, when the door swung open and Dad burst in. He was wearing blue striped pajamas, the top of which hung open, revealing his pot belly. And his graying brown hair was standing straight up from his having been asleep. "What the heck is going on?" he yelled.

We stopped then, as much from exhaustion as from his arrival. We were both breathing hard.

"Well? What's this all about?"

Sandy looked at me, but I turned to stare at the wall. I was not going to take the blame for this one.

"I started it," Sandy finally said.

"Why?"

"I—I don't know. I'm sorry, Dad. I—I guess I just wasn't thinking."

"If it happens again, you'll find yourselves in a lot of trouble! Now get to bed! And if it does happen again, you'd sure better have a better good reason why!"

He left, and Mom came in to see if we were hurt.

"I don't understand this," she said in a worried voice. "You boys have never fought each other. You've always been such good friends. I don't know what...." Her voice trailed off as she looked sadly at each of us in turn. But neither of us enlightened her.

When she had put some stuff on the cut near my mouth and exclaimed about the scratches—I told her I'd scraped against a rough board at work—and made sure Sandy was okay, she left, adding as she went out the door, "Please don't do anything like this again. Both say you're sorry and then forget it. Okay?"

She shut the door.

I flung myself onto my bed and turned to face the wall. Sandy came over and stood beside me. "Shane, I'm sorry. I shouldn't have lost my temper. If you don't want to talk to me, that's your right. And I guess it's not up to me to tell you what to do. But I sure wish you'd smarten up before it's too late!"

I lay still.

"You drive me crazy! How do you think I feel watching you mess up your life?"

"Shut up!"

"You scratched yourself on a board. Give me a break!"

"I said shut up!"

"I'll shut up, all right. I'm sick and tired of trying to help you!"

Sandy turned off the light and got into bed. I heard him tossing around for quite a while. I lay still. My mind was the part of me that was tossing. And it wasn't finding a comfortable spot either.

I guess we both got some sleep. Stands to reason. But when I woke up, Sandy was already studying. Of course, that's not unusual. He studies all the time.

Neither of us spoke. I went to the bathroom. After Mom called us to come for breakfast, we dressed in silence. At the table, there was little conversation. On weekends, Dad reads the morning paper. And Mom was only concerned that we got enough to eat.

When he was finished eating, Sandy excused himself and went to study. I knew I had to get out of there because if I didn't Mom and Dad would ask why I wasn't going to work. So I went to the phone and dialed.

Ted's dad answered.

"Is Ted home?"

"Yeah, who is it?"

"Shane."

"Ted's busy." The phone went dead.

I set the receiver down slowly. What on earth was that about? You'd think Mr. Cummings didn't want me to talk to Ted! Of course, Ted could be sick or something, but why wouldn't he have said so? Or maybe Ted had been high last night and his dad was mad about it. I spent a few minutes wondering what could be wrong, but it was a puzzle I couldn't solve. I'd talk to Ted later.

I didn't want to phone Keith, not after what had happened last night, and then I realized I didn't want to call anyone else who'd been there last night. They'd all have something to say about me and Marietta.

There was only one other person I could call. I dialed his number, and Ernie Walker answered the phone.

"It's Shane. You working today?"

"Not till four. Just thinking of going over to the mall. Want to come?"

"Yeah, I'll be ready when you get here."

"Won't be long."

I was waiting at the front door when Ernie pulled up in his mom's ancient Volkswagen. Ernie is okay. I've known him a couple of years. He doesn't have any really close friends, but he doesn't seem to worry about it. He's just...Ernie. About five-ten. Wears glasses. Not athletic. Nobody you'd ever notice in a crowd, except maybe if you went by color. Ernie's mom is white, but his dad is black. I guess that's the main reason he's on the fringes like me. I find him kind of comfortable to be around. Like an old pair of sweat pants. He's maybe the only person who's never tried to change me.

"How'd it go last night?" he asked.

I groaned. "Don't talk about it."

"That bad?"

"Worse."

"What happened?"

"Nothing important."

"Have you talked to Ted?"

"I just tried to. His old man answered and more or less hung up on me. What gives?"

"Ted phoned me this morning. I guess he flunked the math test and old man Reynolds phoned his dad last night to tell him if Ted doesn't do some work in a hurry he's not going to pass. So Ted's dad got all fired up and grounded Ted until his marks are better. And he especially isn't to have anything to do with you. It seems you're a bad influence." Ernie glanced sideways to catch my reaction.

I slumped further down on the seat. "Oh, man. What does he think I do? Keep his sweet little kid from studying?"

Ernie laughed. "Neither one of you opens a book if you can help it. Did you pass the test?"

"Yeah." A pause. "I cheated. How about you?"

"You forget. I studied right after school so I could go out with you guys that night with a clear conscience. I received the high mark of 68."

"That's nothing. My perfect brother got a near-perfect mark of 97. Of course, he studies all the time."

"Somebody has to get the good marks."

I just looked at him.

Soon we were at the mall, where we bought Cokes. After that, we wandered around until lunch time. I bought a couple of tapes I'd been wanting. We had hamburgers, and then went to an arcade. I told Ernie about my getting fired and Marietta's dumping me. He didn't say much. But he didn't tell me it was all my fault, like Sandy would have.

At last, Ernie looked at his watch. "You know it's nearly four?"

"You have to go to work now?"

"Yeah. Mr. Golachi isn't very happy if we're late."

"So what'll he do—fire you?"

"Probably not, but I'm not planning to find out. You coming now?"

"Guess so. Nothing else to do."

We walked out to the car and Ernie dropped me at my house. I went inside slowly, wondering if Sandy was home. Dad was sitting in the living room watching TV. He looked up as I came in. "You're early, aren't you? You don't usually get back from work until after five."

I hung up my jacket before answering. "We finished what had to be done."

"Oh? That's unusual." But he went back to the TV.

I walked into the kitchen and found Mom making a pudding for supper.

"You're early," she said.

"Yeah, I know. Where's Sandy?"

"Upstairs. He's studying now because of the game tomorrow."

I went upstairs. Sandy was sitting at his desk writing. He didn't look up.

I took off the sweatshirt I had been wearing and got a blue shirt out of the closet. I could look good if I wanted, too. I put the shirt on, leaving the top buttons undone. Then I got a gold chain out of my top drawer.

"You have a date?" Sandy asked.

"Naw, I'm getting dressed up for you."

"You haven't forgotten about the English test Monday, have you?"

"How could I forget when I've got you to remind me?"

"Have you studied?"

"You worry too much."

"Yeah? Well, you don't worry enough."

"Says you."

"I heard you cheated on the math test."

"Who told you that?"

"Never mind."

"Got your spies following me, have you?"

"You're asking for trouble."

I forced myself to laugh, "Well, as long as you keep your suspicions to yourself, I'll be all right." I started for the door, then remembered I had spent most of my money. "By the way, I need some more cash. Lend me twenty bucks."

"You already owe me thirty."

"So now I'll owe you fifty."

Sandy slowly shook his head.

"Okay, if that's the way you want it, I'll get the money some other way." I let the door slam behind me as I went out.

Downstairs, I went into the kitchen. I could hear the TV and I assumed both my parents were watching it. I made a peanut butter sandwich and went to the phone. Ted and I had planned to go driving tonight, but that was out. Ernie was at work. Marietta would be with Keith. Not that I cared. But I had to get out of the house. I looked on the hook for the keys to my car, but Dad must have put them somewhere else.

Then I saw Mom's purse on the counter behind some cans of juice that were waiting for somebody to take them to the basement. Her set of keys would be in it. Did I dare take Dad's car? He and Mom didn't look like they were going any place. And if Sandy was going to study all evening, no one might ever know the car was gone. But it would be just like Sandy to decide to go for a Coke after his work was done. And if he told Dad.... I thought hard. There had to be something I could do. Remembering last night, I reached for the phone book to look up Janice Hopkin's number.

Mom called out, "Who's in the kitchen?"

"I'm just phoning somebody," I called back.

"Haven't you got homework to do, like Sandy?"

"I've got most of it done," I lied. I dialed Janice's number and waited impatiently while the phone rang once, twice, three times. Finally, a female voice answered.

"Janice?"

"I'll get her."

I waited, clenching and unclenching my fist, until at last she came.

"Hi, it's Shane. Remember me?"

"Of course I remember you. What would you like?"

"I wondered if you've still got the car."

"Depends on what I want it for."

"I was thinking in terms of pizza and a movie. I'd pick you up, but like I said, I've got a bit of a problem there."

"Just a second, okay?"

I waited, wondering what she was doing. If she had to ask her parents, they'd likely say no. Then I'd just have to take Dad's car and worry about the consequences later.

"Shane?"

"Yeah?"

"I'll pick you up in about twenty minutes, if that's okay."

"I'll be outside."

"See you."

I finished my sandwich and then tried to figure out how I could get some money. I had just about decided to make up some excuse when I remembered Mom's purse. I opened her wallet. There was a twenty in it, along with some smaller bills.

I took the twenty and put the purse back where it had been. It wasn't the first time I'd borrowed money from her. And although I figured she must have wondered, she'd never said anything.

Ten minutes later, Janice arrived in the station wagon and I got in the passenger side.

"Where to?" she asked.

"Golachi's pizza place. You know where it is?"

"Sure." She drove carefully. "Going to the big game tomorrow?"

I groaned. "Can't you find something else to talk about?"

"Sandy's playing, isn't he? How come you don't play basketball?"

"What do you want on your pizza?"

The subject was changed and she didn't bring up basketball again. We arrived at the pizza place and I got a large pizza and some pop from Ernie, who gave me a thumbs up sign and made a dumb comment about my not wasting any time finding a nice nurse to take care of my broken heart.

Later, I directed Janice to a parking spot near the theater. As before, I came around to open her door.

"Not so hard this time?" she teased.

"What?"

"Being driven by me."

"Don't think I'm thrilled about it."

"Maybe not, but you're being very good."

"Come on, we're missing the start of the movie." I pulled her out.

Inside, I bought tickets, drinks, and a big box of popcorn. I gave Janice the box of popcorn to hold, and then settled down with my arm on the back of her chair. The movie was a detective story with lots of chase scenes and beautiful women. It was only so-so. I tried to liven it up by making comments. Once or twice I got dirty looks from other people, but Janice seemed to think my one-liners were better than the movie's dialogue.

When it was over, we walked slowly back to the car, my arm around her waist.

"Like it?" I asked, looking down at her.

She matched her steps to mine and let her head rest against my arm. "I like being with you."

"Yeah?"

"Yes."

At the car, I took her keys and opened the driver's door. "Want me to drive?"

"Giving up just isn't in your vocabulary, is it?"

"You're chicken."

She reached up to put her arms around my neck. "Shane, sweetie, if I were going to let anybody drive it would be you."

I kissed her, and then let her get behind the wheel.

When I had gone to the other side, I stretched out. "Okay, babe, drive me home."

She laughed and started the car. In a minute we were arguing about whether the hero was hard-boiled (her idea) or merely wooden (my opinion).

At my house, Janice stopped the car and nestled against me. I kissed her a couple of times, and she snuggled closer. "So tell me all about why you don't want to talk about the basketball game," she said softly.

The glow from a streetlight allowed me to look into her sparkling eyes. "That was below the belt."

"Why?"

"Because I got kicked off the team two months ago."

"Oh. Sore spot, huh?"

"Coach didn't like me."

"How come?"

"I missed a couple of practices. And he said I wasn't trying hard enough."

"Tough."

"Just as well. I didn't have time, what with my job and all."

"You have a job?"

"Had."

"You don't have it now?"

"No. I quit. It was boring."

"So, are you going to the game?"

"No."

"You could go with me."

"Yeah, I guess I could."

"I have to go now. Call me tomorrow?"

"Yeah, sure." I kissed her again before getting out of the car and watching as she drove off. Compared to Marietta, she was just a kid. But a nice kid. She made me feel good.

But I didn't feel so good when I walked into my room and Sandy said, "You told Mom you'd already studied for the test Monday."

"So?"

"You haven't, have you?"

"You need to ask?"

"Why do you lie?"

"I suppose you told her I lied?"

"No, I didn't say anything. But if you're planning on cheating again, I might. You're only cheating yourself."

"They should hire you to give lectures. 'Now, boys, you must all be perfect like I am, and then everyone will be happy'."

"Shane—"

"Just shut up and leave me alone, okay? I don't need you or anybody else telling me how to run my life!"

Sandy stared at me for a moment and then walked out of the room. I got ready for bed.

Neither of us spoke again that night, or the next morning. Sandy went down for breakfast, but I stayed in bed.

The first thing I knew, my dad came up to talk to me.

"I ran into Alex Kaufmann last night at the bowling alley."

I buried my face in the pillow.

"He told me he fired you. Said your attitude the last few months has been getting worse and worse. You can imagine how stupid I felt not having a clue what he was talking about. I felt like an idiot. I guess you didn't think you needed to mention it, eh? Thought you could just keep lying to us and we wouldn't find out. What were you going to do? Go into hiding? Or did you think you'd find another job. You're really a prize son, aren't you!"

"Get off my back!"

4

"I'll get off your back all right!" Dad said angrily. "But first I'll tell you this. You get caught lying again, or you fail any more tests, or you get into any kind of trouble, and I'll keep your car keys for another month! Maybe two or three! I don't know what's gotten into you, and I don't just mean the speeding tickets, either. You've never been an easy kid to figure out, but it's getting worse. Not coming home for meals, going out without telling us where you're going, getting drunk, and who knows what else! I don't know what you think you're doing, but as long as you're living in this house you're going to do as your mother and I tell you! Is that understood? And you better get your grades up or else!"

My father's words hung in the air between us and I hovered on the rim of saying, "Then I'll get out of your house." But the little kid in me held back. Instead, I forced myself to pick up a book from the floor. "If I'm going to get my marks up, I've got homework to do now."

Satisfied, Dad left.

Tears of anger filled my eyes, and I slammed the book down just as Sandy came in. I quickly reached for the book again and sat on the bed, pretending to read.

"You started licking his boots yet?" I said.

"What's that supposed to mean?"

"Don't you suck up to him the way you do to the teachers at school? You make me sick!"

"Shane—"

I slammed the book down for the second time and stood up. "All right, you got what you wanted. He knows I got fired, and if I fail another test, I lose my car for a month.

"So you ought to be satisfied. Now shut up and leave me alone!"

"I didn't—"

"Shut up or I'll finish what I started Friday night, and I don't care if he does throw me out of the house. Maybe I'll leave anyway."

"Shane—" Sandy stepped back when he saw the look on my face. "Okay. But it isn't the way you think. And I didn't say anything to him. I swear."

I grabbed several books and a binder and started for the door.

"Where are you going?"

"To the basement where I can study."

"Do you want some help?"

"I'd rather fail by myself than pass with your help." I shut the door with more force than was necessary, and went down to the basement where I spent a couple of frustrating hours staring at my English texts. The truth was I'd spent so little time with the books that I didn't even know how to go about figuring a way to cheat. There was no possibility I could pass the test.

Not that I cared, particularly. And yet, from the time Sandy and I had been little, our parents had talked about when we went to university, and it had just been accepted that we would go. Thanks to Grandfather Blair, a good deal of the necessary money was in a trust fund in the bank.

The truth was I'd be a fool to quit school. I'd seen first-hand the frustration of my dad, who had earned his high school diploma in night school, and who had worked long hours for every penny he'd made.

But for me to have even a hope of passing, I'd have to work harder than I ever had in my life. And there was still no guarantee I could pass. I swore aloud and put my head down on the desk. Every day I was getting in deeper. What on earth was I going to do?

I went with my parents to the game. I had to. It was the championship game and my dad wouldn't take no for an answer. We were a couple of minutes late. I told Mom and Dad I was going to sit with Janice.

She was waiting in the lobby.

"You got the car?"

She nodded.

"Then let's get out of here."

"But I thought we were going to watch the game!"

"Who cares about the game. It's just a bunch of guys tossing a ball around. Let's go."

When she hesitated, I added, "I'm going whether you are or not," and started toward the door.

She ran after me and caught up on the steps. "Where's the fire?" she asked as she tried to keep up.

"Where's the car?"

"Straight ahead."

"Come on. I want to get out of here before anybody misses me and decides I should stay."

"Okay, okay, take it easy." She found the keys and I unlocked the door on the driver's side. "Get in," I ordered.

She obeyed. "Move over."

"Shane, I told you last night—"

"Now I'm telling you. Either I drive or you drive alone."

One look at my face told her I wasn't bluffing.

"You have no right to say that."

"Okay," I started to shut the door.

"All right!" she yelled. "But I hate you for this!"

As she moved over, I got in behind the wheel. In less than a minute we were out of the parking lot and on the street.

I drove to McDonald's.

"How much cash have you got?" I asked.

She looked at me for a moment, and then said, "A few dollars. Not much."

"I've got two-fifty. We should be able to manage. Come on."

I got out and waited for her to climb through the driver's side. Then I put my arm around her shoulders and we went inside.

I ordered, and Janice gave me her money. When the food was ready, we sat down at a table.

We were silent as I ate my hamburger and Janice toyed with her Coke. Finally, I said, "So, you hate me now?"

"You know I don't."

"No?"

"No, but I don't think you needed to order me around."

"You wanted to go out with me. Was it because you thought I was a yes-man?"

"Of course not."

"So what did you think I was like?"

She shrugged, "Okay, I guess I wanted a guy who knew what he was doing."

"Yeah? You think I know what I'm doing all the time?"

"Oh, come on. You don't care what anybody else thinks. You just do your own thing and so what if anybody likes it or not."

"So, you do like somebody who tells you what to do?"

"I like somebody who's as cool as you are to tell me."

"Yeah? Do girls really get a kick out of some guy bossing them around?"

"If it's the right guy."

"And I'm the right guy, huh?"

"Why not? You're good-looking, you're tall and strong and you've got lots of—you know—sex appeal."

"I've got a twin brother who looks just the same. Why don't you go for him?"

"Sandy? He's a 'yes man'. Student council president, honors student, captain of this, leader of that. He's not a person; just a puppet who does everything they say. He's about as exciting as an eraser."

I laughed. "Your—philosophy?—is certainly interesting."

"Do we have to keep talking about this? You almost seem surprised that I like you."

"Do I? Sorry. I just never talked to a girl about why she liked me before, I guess."

There was a pause as Janice finished her drink. A male voice said, "Hey, Shane, baby. How's it going?"

I looked up. "Ted!"

"Mind if I join you?" he looked meaningfully at Janice.

"Sit down. So what's with your old man?"

"You heard, huh? Just because I'm failing a couple of classes, and I skipped out a few days, he's as sore as—"

He looked at Janice. "Well, you know."

"You grounded?" I asked.

"But good."

"How'd you get out now?"

"He thinks I'm in my room. I sneaked out."

"What happens if he checks on you?"

"He'll have a fit," Ted smiled. "What else is new?"

I laughed. "Sounds familiar."

"I see—" Ted stole another look at Janice, "—that you aren't suffering too much."

"I'll survive," I replied. "Don't you have something you should be doing now?"

"I can take a hint. See you tomorrow in prison."

There was a short silence after Ted left.

Janice broke it. "Prison?"

"You probably call it school," I said.

"Oh, come on," Janice said. "It can't be that bad. I think you just enjoy complaining."

"What's that supposed to mean?" I guess I sounded annoyed.

She looked down at the table. "Nothing."

But I wasn't going to let it go. "You think I complain about stuff a lot?"

"Don't get excited. I didn't mean anything."

"I suppose you don't have any reason to complain?"

She looked at me again. "I think life is what you make it."

"Oh? Now you're going to tell me how to run my life. You think I'm making a mess of that, too, do you?"

"Shane," she said in exasperation, "I never said that at all! I don't even know what you're talking about!"

"Yeah, well, don't worry about it."

We left the restaurant a short time later. I drove to my house, parked, and tossed the keys into Janice's lap. "There you go. Have a nice ride home."

She raised her eyebrows. "Shouldn't I call?"

"Do whatever you want."

I got out of the car and walked inside the house without a backward glance.

But as I hung up my jacket, I realized how stupid I was being. It was like I had this need to make everybody hate me.

I opened the door and ran outside.

She was just pulling away, but she stopped and opened her window as I ran up. Tears glistened on her cheek.

"I'm sorry," I said quickly. "It's not your fault. It's just—oh, everything. Anyway, I do want you to call me. Just ignore everything I said tonight."

She bit her lip. "Everything?" she asked quietly.

"Everything stupid."

"All right. You'd better get inside before you freeze."

"Yeah. Call me?"

"Okay."

I kissed her through the open window, and then she drove away. I watched for a minute, hoping she wasn't mad. Then I went back inside the house to wait for her call. When it came, I felt relieved.

Mom and Dad got home while we were talking, and Dad motioned for me to hang up. I did.

"Where have you been?" he demanded, his eyes cold.

"Getting a hamburger."

"What's the matter? Wasn't watching your school win the championship good enough for you? You couldn't waste any of your precious time sticking around for it?"

"Dad, I—"

"I don't want to hear your excuses. Go to your room."

"I'm not a little kid!"

"Then stop acting like one!"

"You'd better go and study, Shane," Mom said, her voice troubled.

I went to my room. I even tried to read one of my English books.

But when Mom called me for supper I had no idea what I had read.

"Where's Sandy?" I asked as I sat down.

"Coach Wilson invited the team over to his place. But you wouldn't be interested in that," Dad replied.

"Sandy was named most valuable player," Mom offered.

I grunted. What was there to say? Sandy was always MVP.

We ate quietly, with Dad muttering every so often and Mom anxiously trying to ease the mood but succeeding only in making it worse.

When supper was over, I climbed back upstairs and threw myself onto the bed. For a long time, jumbled thoughts raced through my mind. I could hear my parents with the TV on downstairs. I wondered how Ted was coping with his father. And I wondered how Ernie managed to keep on such an even keel. Just luck? Or maybe he had a different personality. We'd studied a bit about different personalities as part of the health program in phys ed. I had decided Sandy was the conformist, I was the rebel. Only what difference did it make? It didn't help me know what to do.

Our term marks would be out tomorrow. My dad would be angry; my mom upset. Sandy would have straight A's, as usual.

I picked up my English book and tried to read it, but in a few minutes I was asleep.

Monday morning dawned cold and clear. I was still dressed, but someone had spread my comforter over me.

Sandy was finishing breakfast when I got downstairs.

"Wilf is picking me up in five minutes," he said. "Want a ride?"

"No."

When I arrived at school, the halls were deserted.

I walked slowly toward my locker. I'd have to go get a late slip—something I'd done many times before. But I saw someone else in the hallway. Ted was there, fumbling with the lock on his locker.

"Forget your combination?"

Ted spun around, saw who it was, and relaxed. "Shane, baby, how ya doing?"

"What are you so happy about?"

"Nothing. Why spoil the day by being down? So my old man's leaning on me, so what? Doesn't mean I can't enjoy life, does it?"

"You're late."

"So are you. And, anyway, what's new about either of us being late? I don't know what's gotten into you lately, Shane." Ted shook his head.

"Nothing's gotten into me.... Oh, maybe it's all the lectures I've been getting about how important good marks are and how you have to have a college degree to get any kind of a decent job. I don't know."

"Are you sure I'm talking to Shane? You sound a lot more like Sandy."

"Aw, shut up. Sandy's—well, we both know what Sandy is. It's just—you do need a good job if you want to have some money."

"Come on, you know there are other ways to make money."

"Not legal ways."

"Sure, there are. As well as other ones. Scott's right. You have changed."

"You talking to Scott about me now?"

"He was with Keith and Marietta and he just said—"

"Never mind. I don't want to know what he said. I wish everybody would leave me alone."

"Hey, cool it, man. You're okay, Shane. Just don't exercise your brain too much. You'll hurt yourself." Ted grinned and then hurried down the hallway before I could move on him.

"You're chicken," I yelled.

The door to a nearby classroom opened and a teacher came out to glare at me. "Don't you have a class you should be in?"

I mumbled something, shut my locker door, and followed Ted down the hall.

I caught up with him outside the classroom, just as a bell rang to signal the end of the first class. I shrugged and turned to walk toward my classroom for second period.

I drifted through my classes, barely aware of what was going on. In history, the teacher asked me a question and gave me a detention because of my "smart alecky" answer. Heck, I didn't even hear the question, but what use was it to say that? The English test was a complete write-off, and I handed it in half-way through rather than bother pretending I was answering the questions.

Term reports were given out in last period. I waited until I was in detention hall to opened the envelope. Fewer people were there to see me cringe. I'd expected two Fs, not three. And the rest were Ds, except for phys ed, my only C.

Because of the detention, I was late leaving the school.

I trudged slowly, kicking snow whenever I found some in my path. My head was down and the sound of the car pulling along beside me didn't register.

But the blare of the horn did. Recognizing Ernie's beat-up Volks, I opened the passenger door and eased inside.

"So, how'd it go?" Ernie asked.

"Just wonderful."

"Not good, huh?"

"Not good, man," I muttered. "When my dad sees this I'm dead meat."

"Too bad."

I glanced over at him. "I take it you did okay?"

"Two B's, five C's, and one D. Not great, but I'll take it."

"Yeah. Nobody can shoot you for that."

"Of course, I did do some work," Ernie said apologetically.

"Yeah, right." There was a moment of silence. "You talk to Ted?"

"Briefly. He is not a happy camper."

"Bad?"

"Judging by how mad his dad is already, Ted figures he's going to burst a couple of veins when he sees his marks."

"Oh, brother!"

"He's thinking of taking off."

"Huh?"

"Leaving. Trying to find a job someplace."

"He's crazy!"

"I'm glad you agree."

"What?"

"Nothing."

"You think I'd go with him?"

"I hope not. But you've been acting funny lately."

"I wish people would learn to mind their own business."

"Okay," Ernie said. "Just don't get any dumb ideas."

"Why shouldn't I? I've got more reason to be frustrated than Ted does. At least he doesn't have a perfect brother to be compared to."

"How'd Sandy do?"

"I'm his brother, not his keeper."

"That's funny," Ernie said.

"What is?"

"Oh, there's a line in the Bible about being your brother's keeper."

"The what?"

"Bible. You know, the book they read at churches."

"I don't know that I've ever been to a church. Have you?"

"Well, actually, I have lately. Since my sister came back at Christmas, I've gone to church with her a few times. She started going while she was away at college."

"How come?"

"I dunno. She just did."

"Weird."

"Yeah."

"Anyway, what's this bit about being your brother's keeper?"

"Well, the Bible says you are."

"Yeah?"

"Yeah."

"So what?"

"Nothing, I guess. Just that the guy talked about that verse one of the days I was there. For maybe half an hour he talked about it. Seemed to think it was pretty important."

"Well, I guess he's entitled to his opinion."

"Yeah."

"Likely he doesn't even have a brother."

"Yeah," Ernie laughed. "Likely."

My parents and Sandy were eating when I got home. I took my jacket off, threw my books on the floor, wished I had on anything but my worn white T-shirt with its slogan "I'd rather be sleeping," and entered the kitchen.

"Well, you're late as usual," was Dad's gruff greeting.

"I'll get you some food," Mom said. As she jumped up, she tipped over her glass of water.

"Sit down, Elise," Dad ordered. "He can get his own food."

She sat down and I picked up my empty plate and went over to the stove. I got what was left of the rice and sausages, took a bit of corn, and sat in my spot.

Sandy passed the salad bowl and I took it.

"Well, you got your report?"

I began to eat, ignoring my father's question.

"Why don't we finish supper first, Dad?" Sandy suggested quietly.

"What have you got to worry about? I've already seen yours, haven't I? Straight A's. Just what I like to see. The kind of marks you need," he stared pointedly at me, "to get into a good college."

I continued to eat, concentrating on chewing the food thoroughly before I swallowed.

"Of course," Dad continued, "some of us don't seem to see the importance of getting a diploma. But if I hadn't struggled to get one, we wouldn't be living where we are now. Maybe it isn't the Waldorf, but it sure beats the place I grew up in."

I refused to rise to the bait. I would finish supper first.

"It's...it's awfully cold out today," Mom said. "Joanne Bertram told me her cat would only stay out for thirty seconds."

"Elise, we aren't interested in Joanne Bertram's cat."

"I'm sorry. But it was cold out. Shane had to walk, too. It seems a shame, with his car just sitting in the garage..."

"And it's staying there."

Finally, I pushed back my chair and said, "What's for dessert?"

"Nothing until I've seen your report," Dad replied, pushing his own chair back and crossing his arms.

5

I stared at him, then stood up. "Okay, if that's the way you want it." I went out to the hallway, tossed my books around until I found the crumpled envelope, and returned to the kitchen. "It's all yours," I said defiantly, and then I walked back to grab my jacket and go out the front door.

I walked several blocks, uncertain as to what I should do. I knew I would be in for a tongue-lashing when I went home and that walking out had only made it worse. But I couldn't bring myself to go back.

I walked by Ernie's and thought of going to the door, but somehow I didn't feel right about that. Ernie was happy; why spread gloom around?

I could go over to Ted's, but chances were good Ted's dad wouldn't let me in.

I found myself walking to Marietta's house. The lights were on. I got as far as the front door, and then walked away. A week ago there'd have been no question that's where I'd go. But I had no business there now.

So I walked past. The simple truth was I had no place to go. There wasn't anyone I could talk to who wouldn't just tell me how dumb I was acting. Nobody who would accept me the way I was and just let me be me.

Except maybe Janice. But her house was a good thirty-minute walk, and I was already half frozen.

In the end, I started back home. May as well get it over with. And if Dad ended up by throwing me out, maybe I would go somewhere with Ted.

I opened the door and the heat from the living room hit me. It was followed by the ice in my dad's voice as he came into the hall. "Get your butt over to a chair!"

As I hesitated, he said, "Move it!"

I kicked off my running shoes and removed my jacket. Because my hands were frozen, I had trouble getting the jacket onto a hanger.

Finally, I sat down on a chair in the living room. My mother was there, too, crouched in another chair, holding her knitting to her chest.

Dad stood above me. "Well, what have you got to say for yourself?"

I stared at my feet, which were thrust out and crossed in front of me.

Dad waited only a second, then kicked under my legs, forcing my head to whip back. "I asked you a question!"

I swallowed hard. "What do you expect me to say?"

"What's wrong with you? That's what I want to know? What in blazes is wrong with you?"

"Nothing's wrong with me!"

"Something must be! You don't care what kind of grades you get or what people think of you!"

"There's more to life than grades."

"Yeah! Like what? I don't see you being voted class president! I don't see you going around with the best kids or getting voted MVP! I don't see you doing anything except getting into trouble!"

I passed my hand over my mouth. How was I supposed to answer that? It was true. Compared to Sandy, I was the dark twin. Sandy was everything good and I was everything bad.

"So what am I supposed to do about it?" I asked, tossing my head to keep back the tears that threatened.

The back of Dad's hand caught me hard across the mouth, and I flinched. Tears stung my eyes.

"Walt!" Mom cried out.

I put my hand to my face and looked at Dad.

"Go to your room!"

I stood up. Mom hurried over with a Kleenex to wipe the blood from the cut that had reopened. I spun away from her and made for the stairs.

"Shane!" Dad's voice stopped me, but I didn't turn around. "I didn't mean to do that. But—you deserved it. You don't know how exasperating you are. I can't get through to you!"

I continued up the stairs. I could hear my mother crying. But there was nothing I could do about it.

Sandy glanced up when I entered the bedroom, but he quickly looked back at the book he was reading.

I stomped around getting ready for bed. But making noise did nothing to abate the surging anger inside.

Anger at what? In spite of myself, I understood how my father felt, and I honestly couldn't blame him for his reactions. The truth was I wasn't the son he wanted—Sandy was. It was just too bad that Sandy had been a twin. A fluke of nature.

I brushed my teeth vigorously, wincing as the cut on my mouth stung. I had heard all the clichés. "Who said life was fair?" "You made your bed, now lie in it." "You reap what you sow...." But shouldn't there be someone who could tell you what to do? Is this what it was like to become an adult? To have to figure out everything by yourself?

I got into bed and turned to face the wall. My head was aching. Something was going to have to happen. Maybe I really would go away—with Ted if it turned out he was serious. Or... what? What was there to get me out of the mess that I'd made of my life?

The idea of suicide flitted into my mind, but I didn't give it any space. There must be something I could try, something I hadn't thought of....

Mentally exhausted, I fell asleep.

Tuesday after lunch, I found Ted at the corner of the school yard, smoking a cigarette and flapping his arms to keep warm.

"How's it going?" I asked as I took the cigarette he held out.

"Oh, just wonderful! My old man caught one glimpse of my marks and hit the ceiling. I'm grounded for the rest of the semester. He's going to talk to all my teachers so he knows every assignment I've missed and every test I've blown and everything I have to do until the end of the year. And he's going to pay for a tutor. Oh, yeah, and if he finds out I've been near you or Keith or the guys, I'm going to learn what happens when he gets really mad. Sound like fun?"

"Sounds like he means business."

"Doesn't it, though?"

"You still thinking about taking off?"

"What do you think?"

"Yeah. Me, too, sometimes. Only...."

"Only what?"

"Well, where would you go?"

"Downtown."

"With all the runaways and the pushers and the rest? No thanks."

"Well, at least we'd be able to do what we wanted."

"Come off it, Ted," I took a last drag on the cigarette and threw it onto the snow. "Use your head for something besides a place to carry your hair. You know as well as I do what the chances are of either of us making it downtown. It's a jungle down there."

"Yeah? Well, maybe I'm tougher than you are." Ted ground his cigarette butt into the snow with his heel. Then he lit another. "If we were at war, people would treat me like I was a man. But just because I'm still going to school, I have to have everybody telling me what to do!"

"Yeah. But beefing about it doesn't help, either. There's got to be something we can do—something we haven't thought of."

"Well, don't overwork your brain." Ted paused, then added, "Heard what Marietta's telling everybody?"

"No."

"How Keith is twice as good as you, and she doesn't know what she ever saw in you in the first place."

"That's nice of her. I could say a few things about her, too, if I wanted."

"She looks good, but she's sour underneath."

"I guess."

"Hey, man, you're not doing any better than I am! Why don't you admit it?"

"My old man hasn't grounded me."

"Yeah? Give him time. And by the way, what's with the bruise on your face?"

I swore.

The bell rang.

Ted threw his butt into the snow.

"I'd sure like to cut this afternoon. You game?"

I looked back at the school. Students were hurrying inside. "I don't think so."

Ted laughed harshly.

"Chicken. Marietta's right. You aren't much fun anymore."

Ted strolled out of the schoolyard and I trudged toward the sprawling building.

I was a few minutes late for computer class, but the teacher was also late, so for once I didn't get yelled at.

After school, I grabbed my books and cleared out before I saw anyone I knew.

But once home, I paced through the empty rooms, glad Mom was out. Then I realized Sandy would come in any minute. And Sandy was bound to say something.

I put my jacket back on and went outside. I needed room. Needed to get away from people who were always on my case.

Eventually, I found myself at Ernie's yard. Why not? Ernie seemed to want to be my friend, and he never seemed to get upset by things.

An attractive, dark-skinned young woman opened the door and smiled.

"Ernie here?"

"Come on in. You must be Shane."

"Yeah."

There was a question in my voice, and she obviously noticed it because she said, "Ernie pointed you and your brother out to me once. Knew you weren't Sandy because he isn't a friend of Ernie's."

"Oh," I looked around for Ernie.

"I'm Alicia, Ernie's sister.

"Yeah, I know." I realized that sounded pretty abrupt. "Ernie told me you'd come back home to work or something."

"Partly to work and partly to get ready for my wedding this spring."

"Uh, congratulations."

She smiled. "Thanks. Why don't you make yourself at home? Ernie went to get some milk, but he should be back any second. Can I offer you a root beer or something?"

I'd never been inside the house before and I felt dumb going in with Ernie not home, but I decided it would be easier to accept the drink than to leave.

"So, Ernie says you and your brother aren't getting along very well."

It was on the tip of my tongue to tell her that my relationship with Sandy was none of Ernie's or her business, but the words never got said. "Sort of."

"That's rough."

"Yeah, I guess."

"But it isn't unusual, you know."

What do you say when a complete stranger tells you how to run your life? I didn't say a word.

"I don't mean to belittle your problem. Just to let you know it's happened to others. Lots of others. But that doesn't make it any less a problem."

"It's not just that."

"Not what? Your brother?"

"Yeah. I mean, it isn't him at all. He's fine. It's me. Nothing I do is right." I guess I'd gone so long without having anyone to pour out my feelings to that her interest turned on a tap inside me, and, embarrassed or not, I could no more hold back the words than I could have jumped onto the ceiling. "Everything I do seems to make things worse. I want to give up and get away, only I don't know...it could be worse out there."

"Growing up is rough."

I leaned toward her. "I don't know why I said all that. Just forget it, okay?"

"It's okay. Sometimes it's easier to talk to a stranger. I won't tell anybody. And besides, it isn't as if I've never had any problems."

Something about her made me relax. I settled back in the chair and stretched my legs out in front. "You have problems?"

She nodded. "Not any more. I mean, not bad ones. But I used to think I was the most horrible person around—ugly, unlovable, stupid, clumsy....And then, as you may have noticed, I didn't fit in anywhere. Mom's ancestry is English and Irish, and Dad's is African. I'm not African-American and I'm not, well, white-American either. So I didn't feel I belonged to anyone."

I didn't say anything.

"But I found an answer," she continued.

I raised my eyebrows.

"At university. I discovered God."

"God?"

"You know, Big Guy in the Sky?"

"I don't know much about him."

"Neither did I. But I found out that when you think nobody cares, he's right there, just waiting for us to call on him. And he's got real answers, too."

The back door swung open and Ernie, his arms full of milk containers, blew in.

"Hi," he said. He went to set the containers on the table before taking off his snowy boots. Alicia complained and he stuffed snow down her neck. She screamed, and they tussled for a minute. Then they both laughed, and Ernie went to take off his boots and jacket.

Alicia wiped the back of her neck before turning to me.

"Has Ernie told you what he did?"

Mystified, I shook my head.

Ernie came back into the room and Alicia teased him,

"How come you haven't told Shane what you did?"

Ernie turned his face away. "I will when I'm ready."

"Chicken," his sister laughed. "Well, I've got a dress to hem so I can wear it tonight. See you later, Shane. Don't forget to watch the casserole, Ernie."

I waited until Alicia had left the room and Ernie had poured himself a glass of root beer.

"So what's the secret?" I asked lazily.

"It's no secret. Just not something you'd be interested in."

"Sounds like you don't want to tell me."

"You'll think I'm weird."

"No problem. I already do."

"Thanks."

"You're welcome."

Neither of us spoke for a minute.

I stood up. "Guess I'll go."

"You don't have to. Why'd you come?"

"No reason. Just walking by."

"Sit down."

I sat and stretched out.

"You talk to Ted?" Ernie asked after a moment's silence.

"A bit."

"Shane, I've never told you how to run your life, have I?"

"Doubt if I'd listen to you if you did."

"Well, will you listen to this?"

"I guess." I studied the room. It was small and crowded. Pictures and stuff around. Cluttered but not messy. But nice. Just like Ernie. Comfortable.

"Shane, I did something Friday night. I didn't have to work, and I didn't really want to go to the party at Scott's, and I didn't have anything else to do. Alicia and her fiancé were going to this concert, and they asked me to go along, so I did. The singer was a Christian—a guy who believes in God and Jesus. Anyway, at the end he asked if any of us wanted to go up and ask Jesus to take over our lives. He talked about the mess we make trying to run our own lives, and how we can turn it all over to Jesus and he'll help us do a better job." Ernie stopped talking and looked over to see if I was listening.

"So?" I asked impatiently.

Ernie took a deep breath. "So I did."

"Did what?"

"Went up and did what he said."

I shook my head. "I gather you did something, but I don't get what it was."

Ernie licked his lips before repeating, "I asked God—Jesus—to take over my life."

"So?"

"What do you mean, 'So?'" Ernie asked in exasperation.

"So...did he?"

"I guess."

"Don't you know?"

"Well, everyone said if you asked him to he would. So I guess he did."

"You feel any different?"

"Well, no, not really." Ernie paused a minute before adding, "but Alicia does. She did it a year ago, and she says her whole life changed. Maybe it takes a while before you notice."

"Sounds weird."

"It's hard to explain."

"I guess. Well, I hope you—you know—it works out okay." I stood up to leave. "I thought you were doing fine without any help."

"Sort of. But everybody's got problems, Shane. Only some people handle them differently. You—you kind of let things get to you."

"Thanks. I'll remember that. Next time I need advice, I'll come to the expert."

"You know I didn't mean it that way. I just thought—well, maybe God could make a difference in your life. You should think about it."

"Yeah."

I left Ernie's, and trudged home. The wind was blowing and it had begun to snow. By the time I reached home, my face was red from the icy particles.

The house lights were on, so I would have to go in and face someone. Be nice just to keep walking, but on a night like this, with no place to go....

Mom and Sandy were in the kitchen. I knew they'd been talking about me from the silence as soon as I shut the door and from the way they looked at me when I came into the kitchen.

"Supper ready soon?" I asked.

"About fifteen minutes," Mom said. She smiled. "How was your day, Shane?"

"Okay." I took a cookie from the jar and ate it. Then I went up to my room and stayed there until Sandy called to say supper was ready.

While we ate supper, Dad avoided my eye. I spoke only when necessary, and then in monosyllables. As soon as I was finished, I went up to my room. Sandy stayed downstairs, and I knew they were talking about me again.

I tried to do some work. Maybe if I could concentrate? But I kept thinking about Ted and the possibility of just walking away from school and my family, and then my mind went to what Ernie had said about getting God to take over his life. Crazy. But it would be kind of nice if it were really true. Because, presumably, if there was a God, he wouldn't make mistakes like I did.

By the time Sandy came up, I had accomplished exactly nothing. He came over and sat on the edge of my bed. "I know what Ted's talking about doing. I've also heard that you're going with him. I want to know if it's true!"

I just looked at him.

"Ted's planning to run off and he's told half the school you're going with him."

I still said nothing.

"Is it true?" Sandy demanded. "Are you going to run off with Ted?"

"None of your business," I answered in a low voice. I looked back at the book I'd been trying to read. Sandy reached over to grab the book, but I held on. Finally, Sandy wrestled the book from me, and threw it on the floor. We continued to wrestle until Sandy had pinned me on my back on the bed. With his knee planted in the middle of my chest, and his hands holding my arms outstretched, Sandy glared at me. "I want to know! Now!"

I swore at him, but Sandy didn't move.

"What are you going to do?"

6

"Yes, I'm going to leave with Ted! Satisfied?"

"You idiot!" Sandy shouted. "I can't believe you'd do something so stupid! I knew you'd started hanging around with losers, but I guess I never realized you'd become one of them!"

"Thanks."

"We may look the same, but it's obvious we don't think the same at all. I want to make something of my life, and you just want to destroy yours. So go ahead! From now on, I won't try to stop you. I just don't care any more!" Sandy got onto his feet and walked out of the door.

I lay on my back staring at the ceiling. I felt numb, as though something had been taken that could never be put back. The final strand in the cord that had united Sandy and me since birth had been irrevocably cut.

Once more, I was aware of that deep pain somewhere inside. With my sleeve, I brushed tears from my eyes. Then I sat up and tried to read. But it was no use. At last I went out for a walk.

When I returned, the house was in darkness. I had forgotten to take my key, and I was afraid the door would be locked. It's a strange feeling looking at your home and wondering if you belong in it any more.

The front door was locked, but the back one wasn't. I quietly went upstairs.

Sandy was asleep. I undressed in the dark, not wanting to wake him up. And I lay awake a long time. When I finally fell asleep, it was only to dream of someone chasing me through the snow, someone who was breathing down my neck and shouting threats.

I awoke when Sandy's alarm rang, but I felt as if I'd only slept for an hour at best.

After Sandy had dressed and gone downstairs, I got up slowly. I made it to school only seconds before the bell went. I sat through my classes in a fog, and twice responded to a teacher's question with a vacant, "Huh?" At lunch, I saw Janice waiting for me.

"What's the matter?" She laughed. "You look as though school is one big bore."

"Isn't it?"

"Well, I guess some of it is. But not everything."

"You're a brainer."

"Am I?'

"Aren't you?"

"Well, compared to you, maybe. But so what? I can't help having brains. Why should I waste them? But that doesn't mean I can't have a good time, too. Marks aren't everything."

We were silent for a minute.

"Want to go someplace after school?" she said at last. "My dad's away on a business trip and I've got his car today."

"Yeah? Sure. We can go to a mall or someplace."

"Okay. I've got a student council meeting in a few minutes. Got to go."

"You're on the student council?"

"I'm president of my class. I thought you knew that."

"No, I guess I didn't. You sure it's me you want to date, and not my brother? He's more your type."

"Just because Sandy's the school president and I'm president of my class doesn't mean he's my type. I told you I thought he was a stuffed shirt."

"Yeah, he is."

"See? Meet you in the parking lot after school."

"Yeah." I watched her walk away. Then I got my lunch and joined Ernie and a couple of other guys at a table. They were discussing the girls' volleyball team, and I was free to sit there half asleep, ignoring everything.

A voice in my ear brought me back to reality. "You okay?"

I opened my eyes and found Ernie staring at me, his black eyes sympathetic under the heavy glasses.

"Just tired," I said.

"Hmm. Studying too hard, huh?"

58

"Yeah, right." I grinned. "As always."

I left the room with Ernie and we wandered down to the girls' gym to watch some intramural teams play a game.

"Ted skipped today," Ernie said. "Said he had a few errands to take care of."

"Yeah?"

"Listen, Shane. I know you think what I told you was weird—about God and all. But—maybe you should give God a try first. Before you do anything drastic. Alicia says you would find a real difference."

I didn't reply. I didn't even believe there was a God. Oh, maybe if I'd ever thought about it, I'd have said I hoped there was some kind of higher power who was in control. Sort of made you feel better than to think you were just some kind of accidental mutation.

But a God who actually cared about what happened to an individual person? It just wasn't logical.

"I don't think so, Ernie. I really can't picture it."

"Would you do one thing for me?"

"Such as?"

"There's some kind of big rally this Friday that's sponsored by the church. I've never been to one, but Alicia and Todd are going, and they said I'll like it." He rushed his words. "Would you come? Just to see what it's all about?"

I was rescued by the ringing of the bell.

"I'll think about it," I said quickly as the surge of students separated us.

After school, I met Janice at her car and we went to the nearest mall and had milkshakes; then we walked around making fun of the clothes in the store windows and discussing what we would buy if we ever became millionaires. We had a good time, I guess. But I felt like a prisoner getting a few hours' pass.

The aroma of cookies met me inside our front door. When I'd hung up my jacket, I went into the kitchen. I should do something about that rip in the leather before it got worse. But somehow it didn't seem as important as it once might have.

Mom was in the kitchen with flour on her cheek and hands.

"Hi," she said, smiling.

"Hi." I picked up a warm cookie and ate it. I knew by the way she kept looking at me and then quickly looking away that she was worried.

She continued to drop spoonfuls of dough onto the pan in front of her. "Want some hot chocolate? You must be cold from walking."

"Yeah."

"I'll make it just as soon as I get these cookies in the oven."

I sat down on a chair and ate another cookie.

"Remember how I always used to make you kids hot chocolate after you'd been outside playing in the winter?"

Before I had time to answer, she rushed on. "Remember that snowman you and Sandy made once? The one that was so tall you went and got a ladder so you could try to put the head on? And then you fell headfirst into the snow bank and Sandy couldn't pull you out? He had to come and get me, and we were worried that you might be suffocating. You were so covered with snow that you looked like a snowman yourself. And all you could think about was getting back on the ladder and finishing that snowman!

"Afterwards, I made hot chocolate and Sandy and I sat here laughing so hard we could barely talk, and you kept asking what was so funny."

I drank the hot chocolate Mom made and half-listened as she talked about things from the past—tricks Sandy and I had played by pretending we were each other, holidays to the beach or relatives, birthdays, anything she could remember that might spark my interest. But my mind was only vaguely aware of her words, and at last she stopped trying.

I went upstairs and cleaned up for supper. Apparently, we were going to a restaurant. I'd have preferred to stay home, but there was something within me that said this could be the last time.

So I got ready.

By the time Dad got home, Sandy was there and Mom had finished the cookies and changed into a dress.

We got into the car—Sandy and I together in the back seat.

Mom and Dad argued a bit about which restaurant to go to, but it didn't last long. The back seat remained silent.

It was the same during supper. Sandy and I maintained a stony silence toward each other. Sandy talked to Mom and Dad about school activities. I spoke only when I had to. Though the food was good, the meal was not a success.

As soon as we were home, Sandy went upstairs and I went down to the basement. I played a game on the computer for a while, wasting time until I could go to bed. If only I could drive my car....

That gave my mind something to think about. If I should decide to take off with Ted, what should I do about my car? Could I find the keys? Or was it better to hang around until I got the car back next Thursday, and then go? But maybe I was better without a car. I couldn't afford to pay for parking downtown, and I didn't know if there'd be a parking spot with whatever place we might get to live in.... But Ted didn't have a car, and it might be a good idea to have one. We might decide to leave the city and go somewhere else.

One side of my mind wrestled with this new problem as the other side blasted invaders and explored new worlds on the computer.

I heard Dad's footsteps on the stairs, and I tensed.

"Shane."

"Yeah?"

"We're going to bed. You should, too."

"Yeah, in a minute."

"Shane?" Dad's voice sagged.

"Yeah?"

"I wish I knew what to say to you. You're like a stranger. My own son like a stranger."

I glanced at the man standing across the room from me and was shocked by how old he looked. Had I done that to him? It didn't seem right, somehow. But I didn't speak, because there was nothing I could say.

Dad went slowly back upstairs, and a few minutes later I followed.

Sandy was in bed reading. He looked up when I entered the room, but ignored me.

I got ready for bed, and soon the room was in darkness.

"Shane." Sandy's voice came out of the darkness.

"What do you want?"

"Do you have any idea what kind of mess you're going to get into?"

I put my pillow over my head and eventually fell into an exhausted sleep.

When I woke up, Sandy was gone and I knew I'd overslept. My watch said it was 8:45. Five minutes to get to school. No way. I went back to sleep. When I woke up again, it was 11:30. This was Thursday, so Mom was at her part-time job at the library. Well, I'd have lunch and go to my afternoon classes. There wasn't much else to do.

I got to school as the bell rang, so I hurried in. But there was a substitute and it was a complete waste of time. I almost left after the class, except my English teacher saw me and walked to the classroom with me. McNeely was the teacher I most disliked because he was the teacher who took the most notice of me. He was always writing little notes like, "You can do better than this," on my work, or hauling me out of the room and lecturing me when I goofed off. It was as if he thought he knew me better than I knew myself.

Today, we were given an assignment—to write a short story of at least a thousand words. For a long time, I sat there wishing I had skipped school completely. Then I noticed McNeely was getting up, and knew instinctively he would be coming to ask me why I wasn't working. I opened a notebook, found a pen, and began to write any words that came into my head.

I was still writing when the bell rang, and I ignored it so I could finish the thought I was on. Funny. Once I'd started, the words had poured out. I'd have to read it when I got home and see if it made any sense.

In the hallway after class, I saw Ernie and pretended I was in a hurry. A casual wave, and then I was gone. I didn't want Ernie talking to me about God again.

I walked over to Ted's apartment and listened at the door. If Ted's dad was at home, there was no point in even knocking. But I heard no voices, so I knocked quietly.

Ted's voice said, "Yeah?"

"It's Shane."

Ted unlocked the door, and I went inside.

"Your old man isn't around, is he?"

"Naw. He had to go out of town for a couple of days. Things couldn't be better."

"So what have you been doing?"

"Nothing much. I just didn't feel like going to school today. I mean, what's the point? I'm going to fail anyway. I've been making plans for taking off."

"You're really going to go?"

"Why not? What is there for me here?"

I was silent.

"Want a beer?" Ted asked.

"I guess."

Ted got a couple from the fridge. He laughed. "My dad stocked up day before yesterday—before he found out he had to make the trip. Nice of him."

We drank in silence and then had another. I realized that Ted had already had a few, and that we would likely get drunk, but I didn't worry about it. I had been really drunk only a couple of times before. Usually, I never got more than a little high. Being drunk was a funny feeling, and one I wasn't sure I liked. You thought you knew what you were doing, and then later you found out you'd done really stupid things. And your head ached afterwards.

But today I didn't care.

"Hey, I wrote a—a shtory in English today," I said some time later after the TV movie we'd been watching finished. "Wanna hear it?"

Ted laughed and said he did, so I read it to him. It was about a kid who was hunting for something and he couldn't find it. There was a dog in it, too, and some stupid parents. There was no ending, and we thought that was funny. We laughed until tears started coming down our cheeks, and we didn't stop laughing, even when I had to go to the bathroom to throw up. We just kept laughing and drinking.

I woke to a pounding in my brain. Like a little dwarf was mining for coal inside. I stretched and discovered I was highly uncomfortable. Also cold. As my mind grew clearer, I realized I had passed out on the floor in Ted's apartment. Ted was on the chesterfield. Highly unfair. You ought to give your guest first choice of where to pass out. I giggled, and then grimaced as my head began pounding harder.

I struggled to my feet, and the stench of vomit made me feel sick. The air was stuffy, so I went to open a window, and my lungs gasped as the cold air hit them.

My head cleared a bit and I looked at my watch. Ten o'clock. But the sun was up.... My brain reeled. It was morning! I'd come here after school and had stayed all night! My parents—what would they think? Maybe they'd just say good riddance.

Ted stirred and I went over and nudged him. He looked a mess. He didn't awaken, so I went to the bathroom and leaned on the sink. No one had cleaned up, and the smell of old vomit almost made me sick again. I looked in the mirror. My hair hung in tangles, I badly needed to shave, my eyes were red and puffy, my face blotchy, and my clothes looked like they'd been taken out of a garbage bag.

I pulled off my clothes and showered. I didn't see a razor, but I found a comb in my jacket pocket and combed my hair. I looked half-decent, but not much more than that. And I had to put my clothes back on. I'd have borrowed some of Ted's, but there was no way I could squeeze into anything of his.

I went into the kitchen and found a couple of pieces of bread and a half-empty jar of peanut butter. I put the bread in the toaster and then filled the kettle with water. Every movement made my head pound more, but I had to do something, and I'd heard that coffee helped. I found a jar of instant, and made some. I forced the hot coffee down, along with the toast, wanting to gag but willing myself not to.

When I was finished, I gathered my belongings. The pages of my story were scattered on the floor and I almost left them there. But, because they were mine, I picked them up and stuffed them into my bookbag. I put on my jacket, then decided to leave a note. I tore a piece of paper from one of the story's pages, found my pen, wrote a few lines, and left the note on the kitchen table. Then, after one last look at Ted and the room, I stepped out into the hallway.

It was after eleven. I had to decide what to do now. Should I go home? Just go to school? Or what?

I began to walk, but every step I took made my head hurt more. An alley loomed up and I turned into it. I put down my backpack and stood against a wall, pressing my head into the cold bricks. I thought of pounding my head against the wall, but what good would that do?

At last, I just slumped down with my back against the bricks. Maybe if I didn't move, my head wouldn't hurt.

But not moving didn't prevent me from thinking, and thinking was even worse than the pain of the hangover. The hangover would end eventually. But would this pain deep inside ever go away?

I sat in the alley for about fifteen minutes. Then I pulled myself to my feet and started walking. My head still throbbed, but I was determined not to sit there like a fool.

I came to the school grounds and turned in. A police car was pulled up at the front door. Not that that was unusual. The police often paid visits to the school, and sometimes they had to be called because of a fight or theft.

But as I went through the main doors somebody yelled, "There he is!" and the policeman and several kids ran up to me.

"Are you Shane Donahue?" The burly cop shoved his finger in my face.

"Yeah."

"Your family called us this morning. Apparently, you left home yesterday after breakfast and didn't return."

"Look, it's no big deal, okay? I just stayed at a friend's."

"Yeah? You look like it all right. You're under age, aren't you?"

"Huh?"

"To be coming to school with a hangover? You know I could arrest you?"

7

I stared at him, wanting to explain. But the pounding in my head made it impossible to think clearly. I longed to just curl up in a corner someplace and be left alone.

Looking around for help, I saw Mr. Spencer, one of the vice-principals, staring at me in disgust, and a crowd of kids watching me, most of them laughing. I hoped I wouldn't throw up, but the feeling in my stomach told me there was a good chance I would.

"He isn't going to be much use in school today," the cop said to Mr. Spencer. "I'll drive him home."

Mr. Spencer agreed, and the policeman took my arm and led me out of the building. Somebody behind yelled, "Police brutality," as I got into the back of the patrol car and sank into the seat with my head in my hands.

A second police officer appeared from around the side of the school, and then they drove me home. They didn't say much. Maybe they knew how I felt.

My dad and Sandy both came outside when the cruiser pulled up. Sandy stepped back for me to walk into the house; then, in a voice filled with contempt, he said, "You look like something out of a horror movie. Maybe that's what you are. Well, that's all the time I'm going to waste on you. I'm going to school." And he grabbed his books and jacket and left.

Dad politely thanked the police officers for bringing me home, and apologized for having bothered them. As soon as they were gone, he turned on me. "You're disgusting! Where were you? With some girl?"

I started to shake my head, realized that would hurt, and mumbled, "No."

"Where, then?"

"Ted's."

"Where was his father?"

"Out of town.

"Sandy was up half the night looking for you. And the first place he went was Ted's. Nobody was there."

"We were there, all right. But we were likely asleep."

"Asleep? Is that what you call it? You were dead drunk is what you were. Or were you high on drugs?"

"Look, I think I'm going to throw up. Let me go now. You can yell at me later if you want."

I grabbed for the wall, and Mom cried out, "Leave him alone, Walt. Can't you see how pale he is? He's learned his lesson."

"Go on," said Dad. "But don't think you've heard the last of this."

I stumbled upstairs to the bathroom.

"You're nothing but a no-good—" I didn't hear the rest because I was throwing up in the bathroom.

Later, as I lay on my bed, Mom came up with something for my headache. After that, I slept for several hours. At three-thirty, I woke up, showered and shaved, and dressed. I felt a lot better.

I ate some lunch with Mom. She didn't say anything about the night before, but I caught her looking at me as though she didn't know me, and when she spoke, she was very polite—as if I were a stranger.

She left then because she had to work from four to nine. I thought of going to school tomorrow. Everyone would know what had happened. Better to just go away with Ted and never see any of them again.

But did I want to go with Ted? Was last night a sample of what life with Ted would be like? If so....

I watched TV for a while, but it was all stupid soap operas. I figured I had enough problems of my own without seeing more.

Then I remembered the story I'd written. It had seemed pretty good last night. Would it stand up to a reading when I was sober?

I found the crumpled pages and slowly deciphered them. It was just about a kid and a dog his parents wouldn't allow him to keep, but to me it seemed pretty good. I couldn't hand it in the way it was, though, so I decided to redo it on the computer, and as I typed, the ending took shape in my mind.

I was working on the final paragraph when I heard a door slam. I finished quickly. Sandy was upstairs, yelling my name. I shoved the pages into a drawer. Then I went hesitantly to the stairs. As I reached the door at the top of the basement steps, Sandy pulled it open and we came face to face.

"Have a nice day?" he asked sarcastically. Without giving me a chance to reply, he said, "Thanks for being such a terrific brother! First you keep me up half the night trying to find you, and then you manage your entrance so the whole school gets to see you!"

"Lots of kids get drunk once in a while."

"Yeah, but most don't show up at school looking like something the cat dragged in and get taken away by cops!"

"I never asked for the cops to be there!"

"You might have known Mom would be hysterical when you didn't come home!"

"I—I never thought—"

"Do you *ever* think?"

We were standing with Sandy at the top of the stairs and me a few feet below. Now, I pushed my way up and tried to get past him. But he grabbed my arm, spinning me around so we were face to face again.

"I said do you ever think? About anyone but yourself? Like Mom, for instance! You don't care one bit for anyone but yourself! Well, I for one wish you were already gone with Ted! All you are is trouble!" As he said the last words, he pushed me hard against the wall. I might have come up fighting, but I felt too sick and too tired to bother.

Anyway, the grown-up part of my mind told me Sandy had a right to be upset. Why should he enjoy having a loser like me for a brother?

Sandy went into the kitchen and, as had been my habit lately, I decided to go for a walk to clear my head. I had no destination in mind, and was surprised when I realized I was at Ernie's. Ernie would know all about last night. Would he even talk to me? I went to the door and rang the bell. He answered it.

"Hi," I said quietly.

"Shane! Come on in."

So Ernie hadn't deserted me. Not yet, anyway.

We went into the family room and Ernie got grape juice from the kitchen. I sank into a recliner chair.

"So, how's it going?" he asked.

"You heard, didn't you?"

"Sandy called here looking for you about midnight. I told him to try Ted's. And I know about this morning.

"Dumb, huh?"

"Were you with Ted?"

"Yeah."

We drank the juice and ate cookies in silence for a few minutes.

"Your folks upset?"

"What do you think?"

"Tough."

"It was my fault. I deserve it."

"Shane?"

"Yeah?"

"Look, you're not a bad guy."

"Thanks."

"No, I mean it. I don't think you want to make trouble for anybody. Not like some guys do. And you're not like Ted, either. He wants to have it all without doing anything for it. He seems to feel the world owes him something."

"Maybe."

"You aren't like that."

"I don't know."

"You want something else—something like what Alicia calls a direction."

"A what?"

"A direction. You know. Something to aim at. A goal to make what you do worthwhile."

"You're going over my head."

"Come off it! I'm tired of you playing dumb. You know what I'm talking about. When you want to change the subject, you always come out with that, 'My brain can't handle the heavy stuff' attitude. I don't buy it."

"Maybe I don't care what you buy!" I pulled the recliner up and got to my feet. "And I didn't come here to get yelled at by somebody else. I get enough of that at home."

As I started for the door, Ernie said quietly, "Shane."

"What?"

"How many friends have you got right now?"

"What?"

"I said how many friends have you got? Keith isn't much of a friend considering he stole your girl. Most of the other guys were Keith's friends before you started hanging out with them, so they'd side with him. How many have you got?"

"I haven't stopped to count."

"Yeah? Well, maybe you should. Marietta's gone, Keith, Parker, Dave, Scott, a bunch of others, Sandy.... Who's left besides Ted and me?"

"Janice."

"Janice Hopkins?"

"Yeah."

"Maybe you should ask Sandy about her."

"What are you talking about?" I stepped toward him angrily. "What's that supposed to mean?"

"Ask Sandy."

I grabbed the front of Ernie's shirt. "I'm asking you!"

"All right, I'll tell you. While you had eyes for nobody but Marietta, Janice Hopkins was making a big play for Sandy. Only he wasn't interested. So now she's making a play for you. Don't ask me why. But you fell for it."

I pushed Ernie away. "You're lying!"

"Ask Sandy. Or ask Janice."

I hurried out of the house and almost ran back to my place. I didn't bother to kick off my shoes before taking the stairs two at a time. Sandy was in the bedroom with the radio on, doing homework. The sight of him calmly working was more than I could bear. I swore at him as I knocked his books to the floor.

"Why do you have to be so bloody perfect!" I exploded. "Nobody comes home from school on Friday and sits down to do homework!"

"People who get straight As do. And then they can go out that night and Saturday with nothing to weigh on their minds.

Now, did you come up here to complain about my study habits, or did you have something else on your pea-brain?"

"Ernie told me Janice Hopkins made a play for you first!"

Sandy's smile reminded me of a cartoon snake who had just swallowed its prey. "Sure, she did."

"When?"

"Last month."

"What happened?"

"I wasn't interested."

"Why not?"

"I've been dating Kathy."

"I'd like to smash your teeth in."

"Why don't you try it and see what happens? I'm not responsible for every girl who gets a crush on me, am I?"

"Why didn't you tell me?"

"Tell you what?"

"About Janice."

"Because I felt sorry for you! You'd lost Marietta and then Janice started to make you feel better, so I figured why spoil it. Why not let you have a little fun as long as it lasted?"

"Thanks a lot!"

"Don't thank me. Right now, I can't stand the sight of you. And if you've found out what you came for, why don't you leave so I can finish my work? Go phone your girlfriend and see if she'll come over and hold your hand."

I swung, but Sandy saw it coming and grabbed my arm, twisting it behind my back. Tears of fury stung my eyes as I stood there, helpless, with Sandy twisting my arm higher. Then he propelled me toward the door and into the hall, shutting the door behind me.

I stood in the hallway for a moment before stumbling downstairs, rubbing my arm as I went. I found myself outside again, but I didn't know where to go. Ernie's words echoed in my mind. How many friends did I have? Ted? Was Ted my friend? Or was he just another loser who didn't have any answers. The truth was he didn't care about me any more than I cared about him.

Ernie? Maybe he was the only friend I had right now. Not that we'd ever been close. But he hadn't shut me out, like

Sandy. Hadn't turned on me, like Keith. Or lied, like Janice. Maybe Ernie was my only friend. What a thrill for Ernie!

I laughed bitterly, and once more found my steps headed in the direction of his house.

He opened the door almost before I knocked. I stepped inside. Then I felt like a fool. How could I have been so stupid? Walking all the way over here to tell Ernie that he had the honor of being my only friend!

I followed him to the family room, and went back to the recliner.

"Well, I asked him."

"And?"

"You were right. She wanted him, but he wasn't interested, so she decided to go after me. Why, I don't know."

"Maybe because you look like him."

"She says he's a stuffed shirt."

"Maybe she wants to get back at him for not being interested in her. Show him what he missed."

"She just may have decided she likes me better."

"Maybe." But it was obvious what Ernie thought. "Shane...?"

"What?"

"Will you come with me tonight?"

"Huh?"

"The church rally. Will you come along, just this once? What have you got to lose?"

What did I have to lose? Only this aching inside. But what use was going to some meeting? I wasn't even sure there was a God. "I don't know," I said aloud.

Then something inside said to me, "So how are you going to spend the evening? What do you have to do that's so important? You've got one friend left, and you aren't even willing to do the only thing he's ever asked you to do. Sandy says you don't think about anybody but yourself. Maybe he's right."

Ernie was looking at me, as if trying to read my mind.

"Look, maybe I'll go," I said. "Maybe. But I don't know if my dad'll let me out of the house after last night."

"Yeah," Ernie sounded defeated. "Well, if you can, we're leaving at seven-fifteen. We'd pick you up."

"I'll see. But now I'd better get back. Shouldn't be late for supper."

"No, you shouldn't."

I was walking out the door when he said quietly, "Shane?"

"Yeah?"

"There really is something. I mean, what I said about God and all. He can make things different. Not like magic or anything, but inside. You do feel different inside. I can feel it a little, but mostly I can see it in Alicia. She isn't the same person she was a year ago. And it isn't just that she's more grown-up or something. She thinks differently. Reacts differently. She used to have a terrible temper. Now she doesn't. And she used to think people were looking down at her all the time, and she doesn't do that much any more either. She's different, and a whole lot nicer."

I opened the door and started out, but something made me stop. I fought back tears as I turned and said, "Look, it isn't that I don't appreciate your concern. I do. Right now you're—you're the only friend I have. And I don't want to lose you, too. Only, well, I just don't know what I should be doing. I—I've got a lot of decisions to make." Then I hurried down the walk to the street, and ran home.

When I got there, Mom was in the kitchen. I went in, and, seeing the table bare, began to set it. She looked over in surprise, but didn't say anything. Dad got home and we had supper in relative calm. No one mentioned the night before. Dad told Sandy a bit about an account he was working on. Mom talked about her day at the library. Sandy talked about the movie he was going to that night with Kathy and some other friends.

After supper, I went to my room. Sandy was downstairs helping with the dishes, so I had a few minutes alone. All the way home from Ernie's and through supper, one thought had been running through my mind. What was I going to do? Should I really leave home with Ted? What did that solve? It left my parents upset, killed my chances of finishing school and going to university, put me at work at some menial job, if I could get a job at all, and gave me a room-mate who liked to drink and party all the time.

If I stayed here, I had to live with a brother who hated me and parents who didn't understand me. I was going to fail my year at school. I had no real guy friends other than Ernie. My new girlfriend was likely using me to get at Sandy. Day after day, I had nothing to look forward to except more anger and frustration.

The third choice, which I had previously disregarded, was to end it all right now. No more pain.

Sure, it would be hard on my parents, but maybe in the long run it would be better than having a kid who continually messed up, or who left home but was still out there somewhere. If I was dead, they would be sad for a while, and then they could get on with their lives.

The more I thought about it, the more sense it made.

Only, what if there was a God? What if when you died there was something after? It was one thing to just cease to exist, but what if you didn't? What if you got what you deserved? I would deserve something pretty rotten.

Did I have anything to lose by going with Ernie? And maybe—the chances were so slim as to be almost nil—but, maybe, there was Somebody who had the answers and could help me.

What I needed was what Ernie said had happened to Alicia—to become a completely different person. I smiled. What I really needed was a second chance at life. I'd sure blown the first.

Only you couldn't start over. Or could you?

I looked at my watch. It was seven. I went downstairs and found my parents reading the paper. "Dad," I said quietly.

He looked up. "You want something?" his voice was hard.

"Yeah. I want to go over to Ernie's. I know after last night I should be grounded, but this is important. I promise I won't be getting into trouble or anything."

"I'm surprised you bothered to ask," Dad said, going back to his newspaper. "Anyway, you can do whatever you like. I don't care what you do any more."

"Walt!"

"I'm sorry, Elise, but I wash my hands of him. He's my son and as long as he's going to school I'll continue to house and feed him, but other than that I've decided he's on his own. I was talking to Matthew Kline at work today. Did you know he had a nervous breakdown because of his kid? He said he had to learn to let go. Well, I'm not going through that. He wants to live life his own way, so I say let him. He never listens to us anyway, so if he has to learn everything the hard way, that's his tough luck!"

I went to the kitchen and phoned for Ernie to pick me up. Then I went outside to wait. As I left the house, I could hear Mom sobbing and Dad's paper rustling.

"I'll give it one chance," I said as I watched for the car. "If I don't find some kind of answer tonight, that's it."

8

A small black Toyota pulled up, and I got into the back with Ernie. Alicia's fiancé, Todd, was driving.

Alicia had said that she didn't fit in with blacks or whites, but it looked like she'd found she had something in common with at least one black man.

Ernie introduced him to me and then we drove away.

"Have any trouble getting out?" Ernie asked.

"No. My dad's decided he doesn't care what I do."

"New tack, huh?" Ernie said.

"What?"

"I meant that your dad is trying something different because what he's been doing isn't working. And don't," he said as I opened my mouth to speak, "try to tell me that was too hard for you to understand."

In spite of myself, I laughed. "I wasn't going to. I was going to say that I just thought he was fed up with me and he didn't care any more."

"If he didn't care, he'd just throw you out. You're eighteen. He isn't legally forced to keep you at home any longer. He's just trying a different strategy. You'll see."

"Maybe."

We drove along in silence for a while. Then I asked, "Where are we going, anyway?"

"Donway Arena."

"That's big!"

"Yeah. Apparently, they get quite a crowd."

We talked for a few minutes about the weather, a new video game, and other things that didn't matter.

Then we were walking, along with hundreds of other people, many of them teenagers, into the huge arena. We found seats that weren't too bad, and settled down to while away the time by watching other people, especially some who were dressed in crazy outfits even for teens.

Then a young guy started playing a synthesizer, another one bounced onto the stage and told everyone to look at the overhead screen for the words to the songs, and the rally was on. I looked at the words, but didn't sing. Ernie was singing, sort of, but his voice wasn't great and he'd never heard the songs before, either. Todd had a good voice, and he seem to know the songs. I wondered how long he'd believed in God and whether his life had changed.

The singing stopped and another man appeared. My interest picked up as the man introduced a football player that I had watched quite a few times. The player talked about how his life had been empty, and how all he'd cared about was playing football and making money, and how his marriage had just about fallen apart. Only he'd asked Jesus Christ into his life, and that gave his life a new meaning and his wife and he were players on God's team now and everything was a whole lot better.

Then a rock group sang. They were pretty good, only they, too, sang about the difference Christ made in their lives.

A young woman came up. She talked about how she had been into drugs and prostitution, and how she had had an abortion, and then she'd felt so bad she'd tried to kill herself. But she said she'd even messed that up, because she wound up in a hospital where a nurse introduced her to Christ. Now she was trying to help girls and guys who were into the kinds of things she had been in.

She really caught my attention when she said, "You know the biggest thing I learned? That you can start over. Jesus says that unless we are born again, we will never see the kingdom of God. Well, I've been born again. My slate was wiped clean by the One who really matters—the Eternal God himself. And no, I couldn't really be born again from my mother. But with God helping me, I was able to begin again. And people who knew me before have told me that they'd never have known I was the same person. I am a new creation in Christ."

She stopped speaking and I settled back into my seat. These people really seemed to believe what they were saying. Had they been brainwashed, or could it possibly be true?

A small flicker of hope burned in my mind. Could there really be something? If so, maybe....

Beside me, Alicia and Todd had their eyes shut, but I knew they weren't asleep. Ernie, too, seemed caught up in what was happening.

The rock group sang again, and I listened to the lyrics. They were talking about getting control of your life by giving over the control to God.

Finally, the main speaker appeared. I didn't catch his name, but from the applause when he came on stage, a lot of the people knew who he was. He looked about thirty, and was dressed casually in pants and a sports shirt. While the other two speakers had been emotional, he was very matter of fact. But maybe that was because he hadn't gone through hard times. He'd grown up in a Christian home and accepted Christ when he was three. To him, believing in God was normal, and everything else was strange.

He wasn't emotional, but he was enthusiastic. He outlined logically, step by step, the reasons why people ought to believe in God, the reasons why we need God, and how to establish a relationship with God. He seemed to take it for granted that every person in the arena, and, in fact, in the world, was born with a need for God, but that people try to fulfill their needs through other people or through buying things, or through feeling good with sex or drugs or alcohol. He related that to the football player who had wanted glory and money and found they didn't fulfill his needs, and to the woman who had used drugs and sex, and again, found her needs unmet. He asked each of us to think honestly about how we were trying to fulfill our needs to be loved and to feel like we had a reason to be alive. And then he said that the only way those needs could ever be completely met was by asking Jesus Christ to come into our lives and forgive us for all the mistakes we'd made while trying to do it alone, and allowing God to work a miracle and create in us a new creation—a new and better person.

When he finished speaking, my body felt like it had been picked up and wrung like a dishrag. But my brain was clearer than it had been for days. It all made sense! I had been searching for something, but I didn't know what. If this man was right, the pieces all fit together! I was searching for God, who would love me exactly as I was, and yet would lovingly help me to become the person both God and I wanted me to be. And all I had to do was ask God to forgive me for the wrong things I'd done, and give him my life to start over with! It sounded so easy!

Around me, people were standing and singing, but I ignored them. All I could do was sit there wondering if something that sounded so great could really be true. Then a voice began speaking above the singing, "If you have never asked Jesus Christ to come into your life and take over, why not do it right now? We have counselors who will answer your questions and show you what you should do. Just come down here while we're singing the last couple of songs. If you want to get your life in order, this is the time.

"Some people think being a teenager is all fun and games, but you know, and I know, it isn't. A lot of you kids out there are in real pain. There are many things you can do to ease that pain, but there's only one way to get rid of it."

I nodded. Then, I stood up and made my way along the row to the stairs. I had to get down there. Maybe this was what I was looking for and maybe it wasn't, but at least I'd go down trying.

I was almost at the stage when an arm came around my shoulders. It was Todd. Together, we joined the growing crowd. I heard a girl near me sobbing, mascara forming streaks of black down her cheeks. A boy with green hair and a ring in his nose stood with his eyes glistening, fists clenched at his sides. Others sobbed quietly or stared as if in a daze. A few were wearing huge smiles.

As counselors appeared and the crowd dispersed by twos, Todd led me to a bench behind the platform.

"Do you understand what you're doing?" he asked gently.

"Not a whole lot."

"Do you believe in God?"

"I don't know. I never thought about it much before."

"Do you agree that you are a sinner—that you've done things that were wrong?"

"Yeah—yeah, no question there."

"And you need help?"

I looked at him for a minute, measuring him. "Let's put it this way. Just before you guys picked me up tonight I was wondering how I would go about killing myself."

"Yeah, that's...uh...I guess you do realize you need help."

"Is it real?" I asked.

"God?"

"Everything they said here. It's not some kind of trick?"

"No trick. But it isn't magic either. Accepting Christ doesn't mean that everything bad in your life will suddenly go away. But it does mean that you'll have resources you can draw on that you didn't have before, and you'll have the strength and power of God behind you."

"So I'll be able to fix things?"

"A lot. But the best part is, you won't be alone."

Tears threatened, and I leaned forward, elbows on my knees, hands against my eyes, trying to hold them back.

Todd put his arm around my shoulders, and I leaned against him, totally losing control. But he didn't seem to care. For a long time, he just held me. Finally, he said, "Ernie told me a few things about you, Shane. I know God can help you, and Ernie and Alicia and I will be there when you need us."

I coughed to clear my throat, but I still sounded hoarse. "What do I do?"

"Just tell God you want to believe him, and ask Jesus to come into your life and take over."

In jerky phrases, I said the words.

Ernie had told me he hadn't felt any different, but that some people did. I did. I felt like some kind of a wave just rolled right over me. At first, I didn't understand, but then I realized what it was. I felt loved. I felt that Someone was telling me I was loved exactly as I was.

I sat up and Todd moved a few inches away. I leaned against the wall behind, stretched my legs out in front and crossed them, and thrust my hands into my pockets. Then I looked over at Todd and grinned.

He grinned back.

"It is real," I said.

Todd nodded, still smiling. Then he got up. "Wait here a second. I'll be right back."

I stretched again, feeling better than I had for days—maybe months. No, maybe better than I ever had. It was as if the ache inside had been replaced by something else—a peace I didn't remember ever feeling before. I knew I was getting that chance they'd talked about—a chance to start my life over. And this time I wouldn't be all alone!

Todd came back with a couple of little booklets and a Bible. "Got one of these?"

"Nope."

"Okay." Todd carefully wrote my name and the date into the Bible, then gave it to me. "Cars don't run without gas, right?"

"Right," I said, puzzled.

"Well, Christians (which is what we are because we have Christ in us) get stalled if they don't keep up contact with God. There are two ways. One is to read the Bible, which is the main way God speaks to us. The other is to pray, which is really just us talking to God. It's what you did when you asked him into your life. Here's a booklet that tells you a little more about how to pray, and here's one for you to read in the morning when you wake up and say, "What happened last night? Was I drunk or what?""

I laughed and took the books. Then we stood up and walked out into the arena. After a ten-minute search, we found Alicia and Ernie. Alicia hugged both of us, and Ernie grinned from ear to ear as he slapped me on the back.

On the way home, Todd and Alicia sang some of the songs they'd sung that night. Ernie and I just listened.

They dropped me off at my house, but Todd didn't drive away until after he'd given me his home phone number and his work number and told me to call any time of the day or night.

There were still lights on in the house, so I went in the front door, took off my jacket, and paused, wondering what, if anything, I should say.

"Sandy?" Mom's voice said.

"No, it's Shane." I stepped around the corner and saw that the Milligans from next door were here playing bridge.

"Oh, it's you," Dad said. "Early tonight, aren't you?" His tone was sarcastic, but I chose to ignore it.

"Come and have some chips, Shane," Mrs. Milligan said.

It was easier to obey than to make excuses, so I took a handful of chips, said I was tired, and went up to bed. I was just about to turn off my light when I remembered I'd left the Bible in my jacket pocket. I'd get it in the morning.

Then, for the first time in weeks, I dropped easily into a deep, dreamless sleep.

The first thing I saw when I woke up in the morning was Sandy pulling on a pair of jeans.

I started to pretend I was still asleep, but then I remembered what had happened the night before.

I sat up in bed and said, "Good morning."

Sandy glanced over at me. "What's so good about it? Am I supposed to get all excited because you don't have a hangover?" He finished putting on his pants, did up the zipper, and walked out.

I punched my pillow as doubts hit me. What if last night wasn't real? Maybe I'd been all hyped up by the speakers, and nothing had happened. I didn't feel any different.

I got up, showered, and dressed. By the time I got downstairs, Sandy had finished his breakfast. He stood up as I came into the room, and walked out without a word. Mom rushed to put toast into the toaster for me.

While I was eating, I remembered the Bible and the booklets Todd had given me. As soon as I'd eaten, I took them up to my room and lay down on the bed to read.

The booklet Todd had said to read in the morning talked about how new Christians have a lot of doubts about whether or not anything has really happened. It used a lot of verses from the Bible to say that our doubts don't affect the reality of what God has done. So I should ignore the fact that I didn't feel any different, and rely on the knowledge of what God is like and the fact that he never lies or makes mistakes or changes his mind.

After reading it, I felt better. Then I picked up the Bible and started to read where there was a marker. It was a book by someone called John, and it told about when Jesus was on earth.

I was still reading when Sandy came in. "What are you doing?" he asked.

"Reading."

"Yeah? I thought you'd forgotten how. Mom says to come for lunch.

"What time is it?"

"After twelve."

"Really?"

"Really?" Sandy mimicked as he left the room.

I quickly dressed and took the stairs two at a time.

After lunch, I went for a walk. I knew that I needed to think about what I had to do to get my life back on track. The first thing was to talk to my teachers and see if there was any chance of getting my grades up enough to pass. Then I had to do something about my relationship with Sandy. And I had to get another job—or maybe go back and see if Mr. Kaufmann would give me another chance. But maybe I should forget about a job until I got school under control.

I was too restless to go home, so I walked to the mall and wandered around for a while. I was looking at computer games when Ted found me.

"You look busy," he said.

"Huh? Oh, hi."

"How's it going?"

"Okay."

"Yeah?"

"Yeah, sort of."

"You thought about what I said?"

"You mean about going with you?"

"Yeah. How about it? It'll be fun, huh? How about tomorrow?"

"So soon?"

"If I'm going to do it, why not 'just do it', as they say?"

"Yeah, but Ted.... You can't just go like that. You don't have a place to stay. You don't know what you'll do—"

"Since when do you worry about knowing everything ahead of time?"

"Since.... Oh, I don't know. But it seems crazy to me."

"I never thought I'd see the day when Shane Donahue turned chicken."

There wasn't much I could say to this, so I didn't try.

"You just gonna stand there?" Ted mocked.

"What do you want me to do?"

"I just called you yellow, and you took it without blinking an eye!"

"What should I do? Knock you down?"

"The Shane Donahue I know wouldn't let anybody call him chicken."

"That's kid's stuff, Ted. This is serious. You're talking about messing up your life."

"Last time I looked you weren't in all that much better shape than me! When did you get so high and mighty?"

"Ted, I don't know how to say this, but there is something else you could try."

"Like what?"

"Well, uh, like God."

9

"What?" Ted's voice rose in astonishment.

"Look, I know it sounds weird, but maybe you should try. I could take you to somebody who would explain it better than I can—."

"You're nuts!" Ted was backing away.

"Ted, I mean it. God can help you."

"Is this Shane Donahue talking to me about God? I don't know what's happened to you, baby, but you've lost it! You're sad, man. Losing Marietta must have knocked your screws loose. Talking to me about God! You don't know anything about that stuff. You're just chicken, that's all, Blondie. Just trying to make up excuses for why you won't go with me. Why don't you tell the truth, that you're yellow? Eh, Blondie?" Ted had been walking backwards down the middle of the mall, with me following. Around us, people were staring, moving out of his way.

Now he began cursing me, calling me a coward in every nasty way that came to his head. But as I kept following him, trying to get him to listen to me, he turned and raced down the corridor and out of the mall.

I followed, but when I reached the entrance, there was no sign of him. I thought of going to his apartment, but what good would it do for me to try to talk to him? He wouldn't listen.

Instead, I started off for home, my feeling of freedom lost in the frustration of my fumbled attempt to tell Ted about God.

Mom said Ernie had called while I was out, so I dialed his number, but he had just gone to work. I decided to wander over there.

Ernie was busy making dough, but he called me to come back to the kitchen.

"Getting ready for the supper rush?"

"You got it." He finished rolling the dough into balls and

began forming one of the balls into a pizza shape. "So, how's it going?"

"I just saw Ted. I even tried to tell him maybe he should think about trying God instead of this idea of running away, but he thought I'd lost my marbles."

"He would."

"Heck, yesterday I'd have thought the same thing. I mean, I did, when you tried to tell me."

Ernie chuckled. "I know."

"Ted thinks running away is going to solve all his problems."

"Think we should tell his dad?"

"I don't know. I don't think it would keep him from going. It might just cause a big fight."

"I guess the thing we really need to do is pray for him."

"Huh?"

"You know. Tell God about it. Ask him to help Ted."

"I thought God knew everything. Why should we have to tell Him?"

"I don't know. But we're supposed to."

Mr. Golachi came into the kitchen just then. "Hey, Ernie, you gonna work here or am I paying you to talk to your friends?" His smile took the sting out of the words.

"Sorry, Mr. Golachi. But I am working. I'm getting the dough ready."

"Sure you are. But it takes you twice as long because both your hands and your mouth are working at the same time."

Ernie and I laughed, but I knew I should go.

"Talk to you later, Ernie."

"Hey, you," said Mr. Golachi.

I stopped and looked at him.

"What are you doing leaving my business without eating some of my pizza? You want people to think you don't like it? Here," he reached into a warming pan and got out a big slice. "On the house," he said as I started to reach for my wallet. "Just don't keep Ernie talking all the time, okay?"

I smiled as I took the pizza. "Okay, Mr. Golachi."

"That's all right. You're good kids. Not out there getting into trouble giving your parents gray hairs."

I left, eating the pizza and smiling over Mr. Golachi's assumption that I was a good kid.

When I got home, the house was empty.

I wandered restlessly through the rooms. There was something I should do. But what?

Finally, I got out my school bag and spread books around. I picked up the science text. Okay. Did I have a hope of passing science? The next units didn't look too difficult, but what about the work we'd already done? No matter how much my marks went up this term, I'd never pull my total mark high enough to get an exemption. That meant I'd have to write the final exam, which would cover the year's work. Could I learn everything I'd missed?

I was reading the book when I heard my parents come in. After hesitating, I decided to go downstairs. But I wouldn't say anything about trying to catch up on my schoolwork. I might find out I couldn't do it, and it was better not to say anything and surprise them than to tell them and fail.

So I went down and talked to them for a few minutes.

Sandy had a date that night. It occurred to me to phone Janice, but I decided not to. I was up in my room looking through my computer text when Mom called to say the phone was for me. It was Janice.

"You busy?" she asked.

"Not very. Did you want to do something?"

"In case you've forgotten, there's a play at the school tonight. Young Peoples' Theater?"

"Yeah, I guess I heard something about that."

"I was going with some girl friends, but one of them can't make it so she gave me her ticket. Want to go with me?"

"Maybe. But I don't think I want to go with a bunch of girls."

"You don't have to, silly. Think I want to share you?"

"Okay. You gonna pick me up?"

"Yes."

"When?"

"Half an hour."

"I'll be here."

I went upstairs to change my clothes and put away my books. Why was I even going now that I knew Janice had tried to get Sandy first? And should I confront her with what I knew, or did I believe she had actually decided she liked me better? That was dumb. Why should she prefer me to Sandy?

I put on my good pair of brown pants and the ivory turtleneck Mom had knit me for Christmas. Then I remembered that Sandy was wearing the identical sweater. Oh, so what?

Mom and Dad were in the living room watching a game show. I told them I was going to the play and Dad grunted. Mom said, "Are you walking?"

"No. Somebody's picking me up."

"That's good. Have a nice time. You won't be too late, will you?" Mom sounded afraid.

"No. I won't be late."

"Not our problem if you are, you know," Dad blustered.

I ignored him and went outside to wait, wondering how I should tell Janice I knew she'd lied.

"Looking good," she said as I got in the car and she pulled onto the road.

"Thanks, but I thought that was my line."

"It's just that from what I hear you looked just the opposite yesterday morning."

"Don't tell me you missed that!"

"Very funny. I'm not even sure I should be seen with you tonight. I could ruin my reputation."

"You can always ditch me if you think that's a problem."

"Maybe I like living dangerously."

"In that case..." I leaned over and kissed her.

"Hey, be careful! In case you've forgotten, I'm driving a car."

"And in case you've forgotten, I don't like being driven by a woman...or rather, a girl."

"I suppose you don't have any trouble kissing your—women—while you drive?"

"None that I can recall."

"Cad!"

I laughed.

She parked in the school lot and got out.

But I didn't budge.

She came to my side and opened the door. "What are you doing?" she asked impatiently.

"Waiting for you to open the door for me."

"Oh, you idiot!"

I got out, kissed her, and then put my arm around her as she shut the door and we started into the school. We found seats about half-way down on the right side.

Closer down, in the middle, was a noisy group with Sandy and Kathy at the center.

I looked away, wondering if Janice was thinking about what she was missing by being here with me instead of getting all the attention by being with Sandy. Was I the runner up or the booby prize?

We settled into our seats and the play started. It was a comedy, and it was pretty good. I relaxed and forgot about my problems for a while.

But when we were leaving at the end, I couldn't help but notice the group around Sandy. They were all laughing and joking, and talking about going to someone's house for a party. Sandy appeared to be perfectly happy. The fact that as far as he knew I was planning to run away seemed to be causing him no difficulty. He didn't need me any more. He had all the friends he could handle.

"What are you staring at?" Janice asked. "Let's go."

"Yeah." I followed her up the aisle and out of the building. If Sandy no longer needed me, I would just have to accept it and get on with my own life.

Janice and I went to a fast-food place and I ordered onion rings and drinks. Then we sat at a table and, with much laughter and many gestures from her, we discussed the play.

But after a while, she grew serious. "There's a rumor going that you and Ted are cutting out of here soon. You aren't, are you?"

"I've thought about it."

"You wouldn't do anything so crazy!"

"Why would it be crazy?"

"If you have to ask that...."

"So what should I do?"

"I don't now. I know you act a bit—well, sometimes you're terrific fun, and I love being with you, but I've seen you look so hard it makes me shiver. You really look cold sometimes—like you hate people."

"I sound like a great catch."

"I didn't say you looked at me that way."

"How do I look at you?"

"You smile more."

"Yeah?"

"Yeah," she learned forward and smiled at me.

"Janice," I said softly, "how come you lied to me?"

The smile disappeared and she sat back. "What are you talking about?"

"You told me you weren't interested in Sandy. But you were interested in him, weren't you?"

"I don't know what you're talking about."

"Liar," I said softly.

She got up and walked out of the restaurant.

I put away the remains of our food and got outside in time to see the back of her car going onto the main road. I started to run, but stopped as she pulled into the traffic.

I started walking. It was a good forty-five minutes to my house. Not something I felt like doing. But I didn't have much choice.

I half-expected Janice to drive back after giving me time to get worried, but there was no sign of her.

As I walked, I had plenty of time to think. For starters, I realized I hadn't exactly chosen a great time to confront her. Also, I remembered that I wasn't alone any more, and that I should talk to God as often as possible.

Well, I could do that while I walked, couldn't I? Or did I have to shut my eyes?

I couldn't very well walk with my eyes shut, and I couldn't stand here and pray instead of walking or I'd never get home, so I'd just have to pray with my eyes open and hope it worked.

I spoke out loud, telling God all about Janice and how I didn't know if I could trust her or not, about Marietta and Keith and my other so-called friends, about Ted and what he was talking about doing, about Sandy and the barrier between us, and then about my term report with those Fs on it and how I needed to get my grades up quickly.

When I finished, I felt better. There was nothing concrete to show for my decision the night before, yet I knew inside that I was different. And I was going to act as though God were really helping me and if he wasn't.... Well, I'd deal with that when I had to.

I got home eventually and was in bed reading my Bible when Sandy came in.

I had finished the Gospel of John and was reading the Acts of the Apostles. It was better than any of the books I was supposed to read for school. What I couldn't understand was why nobody'd ever told me about it before.

"Have a good evening?" Sandy asked with a hint of sarcasm.

"Okay."

"Yeah? I guess it was a nice night for a walk."

How did he find out everything?

I tried to change the subject. "How about you? Did you have a good time?"

"Yeah. Of course, my girlfriend didn't drive off and leave me to walk home."

"Hey, that's good!"

"What did you do? Get close enough for her to smell a skunk?"

"Just remember, we're identical twins. If I'm a skunk, so are you."

"Good try. But I'm surrounded by friends. How about you?"

I clenched my lips to hold back the words that came to them. Something told me that if God was listening I shouldn't use those words.

So I ignored Sandy, put my Bible on my nightstand, and turned to face the wall.

But Sandy had walked over and picked up the Bible.

"What on earth are you doing reading a Bible? That's a good one!" He set it back on the stand, and then he got ready for bed, laughing a couple of times over the idea of my reading a Bible.

I kept my face to the wall, ignoring Sandy, praying over and over for help to know what to do. I must have still been praying when I fell asleep.

I woke up early, and couldn't get back to sleep. So I got up and dressed quietly, then slipped down the stairs and was finishing breakfast when the phone rang shortly after nine. It was Ernie.

"Shane?"

"Yeah."

"I should have asked you yesterday, but I didn't get a chance, so I thought I'd phone. I've been going to church with Alicia and Todd and I wondered if you'd like to come with us. We leave at nine-thirty."

"I don't know. I've never been to church."

"Just come see how you like it."

"Well, I guess.... If you think I should."

"We'll come get you around nine-thirty."

"Okay."

I was waiting outside when Todd's car pulled up.

The church they went to was fairly close and quite big. But it didn't look like any church I'd seen. No steeple or stained glass windows—more like a big warehouse. A sign out front said the worship service was at ten o'clock.

Todd parked the car and we went inside and found chairs near the front of a huge room that was getting pretty full of people. Not that I'd ever thought about it, but if I had, I'd have said that people who went to church were pretty strange. But as I looked around at the people who were sitting there or coming in, they looked perfectly normal.

The service began and I was surprised to find myself enjoying it. The music was good, the man who led the service cracked a few jokes, and the atmosphere was warm and friendly—nothing like what I had expected. I relaxed.

The speaker, who was called the Pastor, was good, too. He read some verses in the Bible about Christians being all part of one body and about how every Christian is needed, no matter how insignificant he or she might feel. I thought it was kind of neat him saying that when he was white and more than half the people were black or oriental or East Indian.

But mostly what I thought was that I couldn't think of any possible use God could have for me.

When the worship service ended, a few people came over to speak to us. Then Todd and Alicia led us to another large room, which looked like a gymnasium but right now was filling with people who were getting coffee or juice and doughnuts or muffins, and just standing talking in small groups.

I got some orange juice and a doughnut and wandered after Ernie, who found a spot near a wall, a short distance from a group of five or six kids, a couple of whom I recognized from school.

I saw them glance over, and I knew from the puzzled looks on their faces that they were wondering if it was really me or Sandy.

Just then, Todd and Alicia came over with an oriental guy about my age—maybe a little older.

"Shane," Todd said, "I'd like you to meet one of the house group leaders, Andrew Hwang. I've told him a little about you."

Andrew was maybe five-nine, which meant he had to look up to talk to me. It didn't seem to bother him. "Nice to meet you, Shane. I have been praying for you these past two weeks, and it is very nice to meet you and to hear about Friday night."

I wondered why on earth he would have been praying for me, but at the same time behind him I could see the looks of astonishment on several kids' faces as my name was spoken and they realized it was me, not Sandy. They were no doubt wondering what on earth I was doing at church, especially after Friday morning. I can't say I blamed them.

I said something polite, and after talking for a few more minutes, he excused himself to talk to someone else who was about to leave.

Ernie asked Alicia something about a lady I didn't know. While they talked, my mind flew back to the worship service. In light of everything, I wondered what possible use God could have for Shane Donahue. I couldn't think of any way that he could do anything through me that he couldn't do better through any of a thousand other people.

There was a sort of a dead spot in the conversations around me just then, and I heard a voice say, "Christians shouldn't do anything that would make a non-Christian think any less of Christians."

Another voice said, "Yeah, like coming to school in the morning after an all-night drunk."

I came back to reality to find about a dozen pair of eyes fixed on me.

10

I licked my suddenly dry lips and wondered if I should just bolt for the door. No one who knew me would be surprised. But then I was aware of Ernie beside me. I knew I had to say something.

I turned to face a group of about five kids my age. "Excuse me, I couldn't help but hear what you said. You were talking about what a Christian shouldn't do. I only became a Christian last Friday night at the church rally. So nothing I did before then counts."

You could feel the electricity in the room. A couple of kids were staring at me in utter amazement. A few were looking at the floor, as if embarrassed by what I'd said.

Andrew Hwang broke the spell by coming to my side and putting an arm around my shoulders. "Very true, Shane. A new Christian has a clean slate in God's eyes. But," his eyes swept the small group around us, "how about in people's?"

A few kids looked away. But one or two smiled. One of them said, "Right on, Andrew."

Andrew turned to me again. "I don't know if anyone has mentioned our group to you, Shane. It's a small group of young people who meet each week in each other's houses. That's where we study what it means to be a Christian and pray for each other. And we have fun, too. I am the leader, and there is an apprentice leader as well. She is learning how to lead, and before long she will have her own group.

"We would be very pleased if you would care to join us. Ernie has come out the last two weeks. We're a small group—only six, so you wouldn't have to worry about getting to know too many of us. We meet on Tuesday nights, at seven, for two hours."

I told him I might make it, but I didn't promise.

Like Todd, he assured me that he was available if I ever wanted to talk. He gave me a small business card with his phone number on it and the slogan "Giving hands and feet to Christ's love."

When I walked in our front door, Sandy stared at me in genuine surprise. "What are you doing here?"

I stepped back outside and looked at the house number above the door. "Yep. Four sixty-three. I live here, remember?"

"But I thought...."

Light dawned. "You thought I had gone off with Ted!"

"What else should I think? You normally sleep till noon on Sunday. Why else would you have gone out? Anyway, you told me you were leaving with him!"

"And I thought I've never told a lie!"

"What's the matter? Figured you had it too easy here? Or did you just not want to make it better for me?"

I took off my jacket and ignored Sandy. Dad and Mom were standing in the living room doorway

"Shane!" Mom said. "You're home!"

"Where've you been?" Dad asked angrily.

I had to struggle to keep my voice even. "Church," I said. "Mom, is it okay if I make a sandwich?"

I started toward the kitchen, leaving my parents and Sandy standing with open mouths.

Mom came in to help me make the sandwich. I started to tell her I could do it myself, but something told me she wanted to do it. So I sat at the table and watched her

"Wha—what church did you go to?" she asked.

"River Heights Community Church."

"Oh. I know someone who goes there. She—she likes it."

"Yeah, it's pretty good."

"Di—did you go by yourself?"

"No. I went with Ernie and his sister and her boyfriend. They go there."

"That's nice."

She sounded so puzzled that I had to fight to keep from laughing. Dad and Sandy were standing in the doorway. Dad looked puzzled, but Sandy was angry.

"So what are you trying to pull off?" he said.

I glanced at him. "I'm not trying to pull off anything. You asked where I was and I told you."

"You can't fool me. You've got something up your sleeve. But I'm not wasting my time worrying about it. Mom, I'm going over to Wilf's. I'll be back for supper."

He left, and I ate my sandwich. Dad was still standing watching me. "So you were at church, huh?" He paced around the kitchen. "Just why would you want to go to church?"

"Well—"

"You got your eye on some girl there, huh? What else could it be?"

I measured my words carefully. "I guess because I wanted to learn more about God."

"God? What do you want with God?"

I tossed my head to get my hair back from my face. Then I looked straight at Dad. "I figured it was time I knew something about him."

"About God?"

"Yeah."

"You don't need that stuff! That's just a crutch for people who can't make it under their own steam."

"Well, I guess I'm one of those people."

"No way. All you have to do is get working on your school-work. You get good marks, get into university, get a good job, enough money, you don't need any God! You don't see me out looking for some God to give me an excuse for failing! I'm making it on my own. And so is Sandy!"

We had both forgotten Mom. "If Shane wants to find out about God, that's not a crime, Walt." Her voice trembled. "There's nothing wrong with that, is there?"

"You suppose I want people thinking my son needs a crutch to stand up?"

"I'd rather he had a crutch than have him lying on the ground!" Her voice was shaking.

"It's okay, Mom. Dad, look, let me do this my own way. It can't hurt to find out more, can it?"

"I don't want you turning into some wimpy do-gooder. You stay away from that church!"

"Dad!"

"You heard me!"

"You don't know what you're saying!"

"Oh, yes, I do. A lot more than you know." And he walked into the living room, turned on the TV, and buried himself in the newspaper.

I looked at Mom.

She was standing in the middle of the kitchen, with one hand in the air like a statue.

"Mom?" I said.

Her face twisted and tears began to come.

"Mom, it's okay."

She shook her head.

"Really! I'm okay now. I'm not looking for God. I've already found him!"

She stared at me. "You mean that? You—you're okay?"

"Yes." As I said the word, I realized it was true.

She gave a great sigh. "Oh, Shane, I'm so glad."

"Yeah," I said, looking at the floor.

"But don't say too much in front of your father, Shane. He—he doesn't like talking about God."

"I can see that."

She nodded.

"Okay. I won't say anything. But I am going to church, Mom."

She nodded quickly. "We'll find a way. Sometime—sometime I might go with you. If you don't mind."

Tears welled up in my eyes. I shook my head. "No," I said. "I wouldn't mind."

I turned and went upstairs.

For a while I read my Bible, looking especially at the verses the pastor had read that morning. I liked the idea of the body. God giving each person the ability to do something special. But could God really use me?

After a while, I realized I had to do some work. I phoned Ernie to find out what homework we had for the three classes we were in together. He gave me the assignments. Then I phoned a couple of kids who were in other classes. Their voices sounded surprised, but I got the information I needed.

Then I got busy. I remembered the story for English and went to the basement to retrieve it. Next, I studied for a history test. Fortunately, the test was only on what we had taken in the two weeks since second term started. That, I could maybe pull together.

Methodically, I worked on each subject, pausing only to go down for supper and help Mom with the dishes. Sandy had phoned to say he was having supper at Wilf's, so I was able to work without interruption. And by the time Sandy returned, I was getting ready for bed. We didn't speak.

I was up early the next morning. Something the football player had said at the rally Friday night had made me think it was a good idea to stay in good physical condition. Since basketball season was over, I had decided to go early and run laps.

I had fifteen minutes to run alone before other kids showed up. I was about to leave when Mr. Thatcher, one of the phys ed teachers, called out, "Sandy!"

Used to being mistaken for my brother, I ran toward him.

"I didn't know you were running!" said Mr. Thatcher. "I'm coaching track this year. You thinking about joining?"

"I'm not Sandy. I'm Shane."

"Oh, I thought it was Sandy." Coach Thatcher started to walk away.

Something stirred inside me, and without considering, I called out, "Yes, I am."

The coach turned, "You're what?"

"Thinking of joining the track team."

"I don't think so, Shane. We're pretty strict. No drinking or smoking, no late nights, early morning practices you have to attend unless you're actually sick, and just plain hard work. Frankly, I don't think you could cut it."

"Yes, I could."

"I doubt it. And, anyway, you have to be passing all subjects or you're off the team."

With three Fs there was nothing I could say in reply to this. The coach went into his office and I went to the shower. There had been other kids watching, and I knew it would be all over the school by afternoon that Shane Donahue had tried to join the track team and been turned down in no uncertain terms!

In the shower, I looked up at the ceiling and said, "Okay, God. Now what do I do?"

No writing appeared on the ceiling, and no voice spoke in my ear. So I was on my own.

"Well, God," I whispered, "I hope you're going to be around when I really need you. Like at that history test." Then it occurred to me that I was being selfish. "It's okay about the test. I guess maybe you've got more important things to do, like looking after Ted. I'll be okay."

I dressed quickly and was at class a full five minutes early. A new record!

Classes went okay. It dawned on me that since my teachers had been conditioned to expect nothing from me, it was fairly easy to get by without being called on. Except in McNeely's English class. There I had to pay attention. But today's class was simple. He wanted us to talk about writing short stories—based on our just having written one. Since I had actually written the story, when he asked me a question, for once I had an answer. In fact, he said it was a good answer.

When lunch came, I found Ernie, and we made plans to meet after school. Later, on my way to my locker to get the books I needed for afternoon classes, I bumped into Janice. Or rather, she bumped into me.

"Oops," she said in a mock-sorry voice.

"Why don't you watch where you're going, babe?" I matched her tone.

"Oh, but I do."

"Like on Saturday night, huh?"

"Did you have a long walk home? I hope."

"Yes, I did."

"Too bad."

"Yeah, I'm sure you think so."

"Oh, I do. And now you know what happens to people who call me a liar." Quickly she put her finger on my lips. "Don't say it," she urged.

"What do you think I was going to say?"

"You know."

"Sandy and one of my friends both told me about it. So why deny it?"

"I didn't lie to you. I told you that I didn't like Sandy. I just didn't say why. And, anyway, I couldn't tell you guys apart a month ago. Now that I've gotten to know both of you, I know which one I want. You."

"Yeah, sure."

"I mean it."

"You mean if Sandy asked you out you'd turn him down?"

"I sure would! But I won't turn you down."

"I wish I could believe you."

For an answer, she reached up, put her arms around my neck, and pulled my face down so she could kiss me, right there in the hallway with kids walking by and whistling.

"Satisfied?" she asked. She turned and walked away.

My stomach was doing flip-flops. She was really something else! I could hear guys making comments—one of them was Keith—but I ignored them, hurried to my locker, got what I needed, and went to my class.

Later, when the last bell finally rang, I gathered up my books and went to meet Ernie. We went for Cokes—on Ernie since I was broke. I had realized God wouldn't appreciate my taking money from my mom's purse.

I wasn't sure if letting a friend pay for me was much better, but at least that was in the open, and the friend had a choice.

"Looks like Ted took off," Ernie said.

"Crazy fool!"

"Yeah." Ernie glanced sideways at me as if unsure of how I was going to react. "But before he went, he told Keith some story about how you chickened out."

I sighed. Now that would be all over the school, too. "So how's your car been running lately?" I asked.

Ernie laughed and allowed me to change the subject. The rest of the afternoon went okay, and I was able to forget my problems for a while.

But during supper, Sandy made allusions to the morning event with Coach Thatcher. I chose not to rise to the bait, so I got through the meal okay.

After supper, Sandy went to the library to work on a project, and I went to my room to work on my math. But I quickly got bogged down. I started to call Ernie; then remembered that

Ernie had a C in math. That wasn't bad, but it meant he might have difficulty explaining it to me. On a long shot, I pulled out Todd's number and called him. When Todd answered, I said, "This is Shane. Look, this is a really dumb question, but you said you wanted to help any way you could."

"Sure I do. What is it?"

"Are you any good in math?"

"Shane, I'm an accountant."

"I guess that means you're good in math."

Todd laughed. "That means I'm terrific in math. Need some help?"

"I figure I need to get my grades up. Math's one of the things I'm failing, and there are parts of it I just don't get."

"I'll be right over."

"Are you sure? I don't want to bother you."

"I said I'll be right over. Shall I come in or do you want to come back here?"

I thought quickly. Dad had gone back to the office and Sandy was out. Should be safe. "Come in. We'll go down to the basement. I should warn you, in case my dad comes in, don't say anything about God. He—well, he kind of got upset when I mentioned going to church. Really upset."

"Okay. I'm your math tutor and that's it?"

"Yeah."

"Gotcha."

I took my books to the basement, got soft drinks from the fridge, and was waiting to open the door when Todd arrived. Mom was knitting in the living room, so I introduced Todd as a friend who was going to help me with my math, and although she looked totally mystified at having this grinning young black man suddenly appear on the doorstep to teach me math, she didn't say anything.

It was amazing how clear the problems became when Todd explained them. Finally, I said, "You ought to be a teacher. You sure make a lot more sense than the one I've got."

I realized how that sounded.

"Not that he's the reason I'm failing. I haven't tried at all. But you are good."

"Thanks," smiled Todd. "Maybe someday I'll do just that."

We worked until ten o'clock, and then Todd left. I felt as though the task of catching up wasn't nearly as impossible as it had been.

Dad and Sandy both came home shortly after Todd left, and I was glad I didn't have to explain Todd to them. I knew instinctively that Mom wouldn't say anything.

The next day was Tuesday. I decided I would try the house group Andrew Hwang had mentioned. Especially since Ernie was going. So I just told my dad I was going out with Ernie. He didn't say anything.

The house group was at Andrew's house this week. An oriental woman opened the door and bowed to us. Then she led us to the rec room, where some kids I didn't know were sitting in a circle. I relaxed. Even though Ernie had told me I wouldn't know the kids, I'd been afraid they'd be the ones from church on Sunday.

We spent a lot of time getting to know each other—answering a few simple questions, like where did you live when you were ten. After that we sang a few short songs—or rather, the others sang and I listened. Then we spent some time talking about what it means to be a Christian, and how God doesn't make everything perfect for his children because having everything perfect doesn't result in you changing. Lastly, we spent time talking about what was happening in our lives and praying about the things people mentioned.

Besides Andrew, there was Angie, a blond first year college student, who was the apprentice leader even though she'd been a Christian for only a year and a half; Doria, a very pretty Japanese girl who was about sixteen and had been a Christian only a few months; Susan, a black girl who was Doria's friend and apparently had helped her a lot; Brad, a high school senior who was built like a football guard but was actually planning to write computer programs; and Hans, an exchange student who was here for six months and had looked for a church before he did anything else. Hans had been a Christian for a couple of years. Andrew and Susan were from Christian families. Brad's dad was the pastor. Doria's father was an alcoholic who had recently gone to jail for beating his wife. He'd just that week asked Jesus into his life.

We spent a lot of time praying for him and his family.

It's funny, but by the end of the evening I knew these kids better than I knew the kids I'd gone to school with all my life. And I felt they really cared about each other and even about me. They all knew who I was because Ernie had apparently asked them to pray for me when he first came two weeks before. And I was surprised to realize that I didn't mind one bit.

I went home feeling like I really wasn't alone any more. Not only was God with me, but Ernie and Alicia and Todd and Andrew and the group were on my side, too. I went to sleep remembering Doria's words: "Shane, you think you've messed up, but look at my dad. Just think what a difference it would have made in his life and mine if he'd realized twenty years ago that God had to come first in his life. Look at all the pain he and my mom and all our family would have avoided. You've still got your whole life before you."

The next few days passed uneventfully. I worked harder than I had in my life before. There was a major math test on Friday, and Wednesday I met Todd at Ernie's and both of us worked under Todd's supervision.

Thursday I came down in the morning and my car keys were sitting at my spot on the table. Just before Dad left for work, he came over to me and looked me squarely in the eye.

"One wrong move and they're gone. And for a lot longer than two weeks! Got it, buddy?"

Resentment flared up in me, but I choked it off. I nodded, and Dad, satisfied, left.

I picked up the keys, thought about the gas money I didn't have, and put the keys up on the peg Sandy had made in woodworking when we were in grade nine. Then, whistling, I left for school.

The day passed without incident, and after school, I went home and studied until eleven o'clock.

The next morning, Friday, I ran laps in the gym again, and once more I was on time for class. I surprised my computer teacher by handing in a flow chart on time. Not only that, but it was done legibly rather than scrawled on the back of a piece of crumpled paper as was my custom.

Then came math class. As I began doing the test questions, I felt strange. I was so used to not having studied, and, lately, to cheating, that it was almost a new experience to find that the questions made sense. Thanks to Todd, there were only a couple that totally baffled me, and the rest I at least had some idea of what to do with. I had reason to hope that I would pass.

So when I went into my last class for the day, phys ed, I was feeling pretty good.

Then I saw that we were beginning a badminton unit and the teacher had paired me with Paul Gregg, a member of the basketball team and a good friend of Sandy's.

Paul and I were up against two guys I barely knew.

I went to my position, we volleyed for serve, and the other team lost. I served. The birdie was too high, and the opposing player easily sent it soaring to where Paul waited. Paul skimmed it across the net onto the line, and we had one point. I served again, and again Paul effortlessly sent the return into a perfect spot. Then I served and misjudged the returning shot. My racquet swept down hard to smash, but all I hit was the air.

"You couldn't hit a barn door," taunted Paul as the opposing players tried to hide their smiles.

My temper rose but I refused to give in to it. So, okay, I had looked pretty silly. Why pretend I hadn't? And if Sandy's friends didn't like me, so what? They were entitled to like whoever they wanted.

The game continued to eleven points. Paul played very well, and we won despite a few more bad shots from me. Then we rested while other teams played.

As we sat on the bench, I watched Sandy and his partner cream their opposition. Sandy was good at everything he tried. And I had to admit he didn't blow his own horn about it.

Of course, with everybody else blowing it for him, he didn't have to.

The second set of games came to an end, and I had to play with Paul again.

I was tense, and I ended up either putting birdies into the net or hitting them too hard and having them go out of bounds. I knew I was trying too hard. What I didn't know was how to stop.

When Paul called me a klutz for the second time, I lost control and started for him. "Yeah, you're such a hot shot, aren't you? Well, if I'm so lousy, why don't you just play them by yourself?"

I hammered my racquet onto the polished floor inches in front of his feet and ran into the locker room.

11

I'd blown it again! Why could I never do anything right? I picked up a towel and flayed it against the wall several times. Then I sank onto one of the benches. Why was I so stupid?

I heard the door open, and knew without turning around that the teacher was standing there.

"I'll see you in my office at the end of class," Mr. Anderson said brusquely. "Be there!" Then the door shut.

I pulled myself to my feet and went to shower. My mind was whirling. Mr. Anderson was going to tear me apart! And what could I say in defense?

Had I blown it with God, too? I'd been trying hard to change, to be more like Todd was, like I knew from reading the Bible what God wanted me to be. But I just couldn't cut it. Did that mean God would give up on me now?

When I was dressed, I went back into the gym and walked along the wall until I reached the coach's office. Everybody could see me there. They'd be talking about me, laughing. Even Sandy. I leaned against the wall, wishing I was invisible, until the period ended and everyone took down the nets and left. It was the last class of the afternoon, so they took their time. But so what? I'd blown it, hadn't I? I deserved whatever happened.

Mr. Anderson was in the equipment room seeing that the nets and racquets were put away properly, but at last he came out, locked the door, and walked toward where I was waiting. He was carrying a racquet with a broken shaft.

I tossed my head back, clenched my jaw, and stared at the far wall.

Mr. Anderson walked past me into the office. He set the racquet on his desk, then walked back to the door.

"Well?" he asked. "Are you waiting for a formal invitation to come in?"

I went past him into the small, crowded office. There were piles of stuff everywhere. I took a couple of magazines off one of the chairs and sat down.

Mr. Anderson sat on the edge of his desk and held up the racquet. "You owe me twenty bucks," he said matter-of-factly.

I stared at him and then shook my head.

"You think it isn't worth that much?"

"No, I just don't have the money."

"You can pay me next class."

"I can't."

"Can't? Or won't?"

"Can't."

"I wasn't aware your family had financial problems."

"No, it isn't that." I stared at the floor, then looked up and brushed the hair from my face. "You wouldn't understand."

"Try me."

"No. Look, I'll pay for the racquet, only...not now. Not until I can get some money."

"What about the racquet you're going to break next class? And the one the class after that?"

"I—I won't. I didn't mean to.... Oh, who'm I trying to kid!" I stood up and turned my back to the coach. I was fighting to keep control.

"I've been watching you, Shane. I'm new here this year, so I don't know a lot about backgrounds and all. Just what I pick up from hearsay. But I look at you and I see one unhappy, frustrated young man. And I look at your twin brother and I see a popular, talented young man. It doesn't take much of a brain to put the two together."

I turned to look at him.

"It's perfectly common in families with two kids close in age that they don't get along, and they often become very different. Only I don't think either one of you is happy."

"Sandy is." The words were out before I could stop myself.

"Maybe. I doubt it. But, for sure, you aren't."

There was no answer for this, and I didn't pretend there was.

"Coach Thatcher told me he turned you down for the track team."

108

I looked away again.

"I think that was a mistake."

I bit my lip.

"You've been coming early to run?"

"Yeah."

"How about if I come and give you some advice? How to warm up properly, how many laps, the right stride? That sort of thing."

I looked at him in surprise. "Why?'

"Why not? No, that isn't a good enough answer. Because I don't think you are what you seem to be. What I hear from most of your teachers is that you don't care about anything, you're hard, and you're going to end up in trouble. I don't buy it. I think you're hard because you're afraid to be vulnerable, and I think you need a friend more than you need another accuser."

I didn't say anything. I couldn't have said anything if you'd paid me.

"As for the racquet, how about you pay it off in workouts? A dollar a workout. How's that?"

"That means you end up paying for it."

"I can afford that much of an investment."

"No. I'll pay for it. I'm thinking of selling my car."

"Suit yourself. But the offer stands."

"Nobody—"

"I'll be here Monday at 6:45."

"I—I'll see." I looked around, wanting to get away. "May I go now?"

"Sure."

I got the books I needed from my locker, and almost ran home.

Once there, I hurried up to my room, only to reel back as I came face to face with Sandy, Paul, and Wilf Jonson. They were in a tight group looking at something Paul was holding, and they were laughing.

"Hey, here he is," laughed Wilf. "Come on in and tell us all about what you've learned."

I ignored him and walked over to throw my books onto my bed.

"Are you going to be preaching to us soon?" Paul said.

Puzzled, I turned to look at him. He was holding my Bible. "Give me that!" I said, reaching out to grab it from him.

Paul tossed it quickly to Wilf, and held out his hands innocently toward me. "What, you want to fight me because I play badminton better than you? Wasn't breaking your racquet enough?"

"Yeah, Shane, what did Mr. Anderson have to say?" Sandy asked.

Paul slid one finger against the other. "Naughty, naughty, huh?"

I ignored him and tried to grab the Bible from Wilf, but he tossed it over my head to Sandy, who held it for a moment while meeting my eyes. Then, as if making a decision, he looked away and tossed it back to Paul.

"I thought people who read their Bible and go to church don't go around losing their temper," said Wilf.

"Maybe you need a refresher course." Paul laughed.

"Yeah, you don't seem to have learned much," Wilf said.

"Is that why you didn't take off with Ted?" Sandy asked as he caught the Bible and threw it with the same motion to Wilf. "Because you've got religion?"

"Hey, don't hit me," Paul said as I tried to get past him to get the Bible from Wilf. "That wouldn't be very nice. You're supposed to turn the other cheek, aren't you?"

I realized I was making a fool of myself, and I also knew my temper was close to the breaking point. I'd lost it once today, and I was determined not to lose it again. So I turned and ran out of the room and out of the house. I ran full speed all the way to Ernie's and knocked on the door. But it was Alicia who answered.

"Ernie here?"

"No, he had to work."

I sighed and started to leave.

"Did you need to talk to him, or will I do?"

I turned back and a grin tugged at the corner of my mouth. For some reason, it was hard to stay angry in front of her. "It's okay. It wasn't anything."

"Mom and I made cookies this afternoon."

"Yeah?"

"Double chocolate chip."

"You talked me into it." I went inside, dropping my jacket on a hook on the wall.

"Mom's gone out to get some groceries for supper, so we're safe to steal a few." Alicia smiled.

"Don't you work?"

"Shifts. This is my day off."

"Oh."

She loaded a plate with cookies, got juice out of the fridge, and led me into the family room. "So how's it going?"

"Lousy," I replied with my mouth full of cookie.

"That bad?"

"Yeah."

"Are you having trouble believing?"

I shook my head.

After I swallowed, I said, "No. The problem is me. This afternoon I lost my temper and acted like an idiot. And just now I had to get out of the house or I'd have lost it again."

"So?"

"What do you mean, 'so'?"

"So what's the problem?"

"Me."

She laughed. "Exactly. God doesn't change. Our problem is that even after accepting Christ as Savior and Lord, we still mess up. But as long as we're trying to do things his way, we can't let the little slip-ups get us down."

"But isn't he mad at me? I mean, well, I blew it. So why would he care about me any more? Won't he just realize I'm not worth the trouble and give up on me?"

"Never. Come on Shane. Nobody's perfect. We all make mistakes, whether we have God helping us or not. Because—let's face it—life is hard. The trick is that when you do make a mistake or blow things, you have to ask him to forgive you."

"And he will?"

"As long as we really mean it, he will."

"So he doesn't care if I blow it?"

"Well, sure, he cares what we do. It's not like we can just go and do whatever we want and then say, 'Okay, God, forgive me,' and then go do it all again. That would be wrong because we wouldn't even be trying. But if we really want to do what God wants, and now and then we blow it, that's okay. Maybe we'll never be perfect, but if we let him have control of our lives, and if we really try to live as he wants, then we will get closer and closer to perfect. You're just at the beginning of the trail, so he knows you'll make mistakes. Probably lots of mistakes."

"I thought maybe I was done for."

She smiled.

"It's hard," I said after a while.

"What is?"

"Not reacting like I would have before. I mean, I'm trying not to get mad and everything, but it seems like everybody else is trying to get me mad."

"Nobody can. We often talk as though other people can make us get angry, but that's silly. You have to allow yourself to lose your cool. Believe me, I know. I used to have a really short fuse. But it's getting longer, because the closer I get to God, the more he gives me the fruit of the Spirit."

"What's that?"

"Love, joy, peace, patience, kindness, goodness, faithfulness, gentleness, and self-control."

"That doesn't sound anything like me!"

"It'll come."

"Maybe. Anyway, I guess I should get back." I got up and then sat down again. "By the way, what does God expect me to do when people are riding me—you know, trying to make me get mad?"

"Treat them with kindness. Oh, that sounds so glib!" She stood up and walked around the room. "Shane, everybody's got what they call their own cross to bear. Mine happens to be my color. All my life, I've had people treat me with disrespect or even hatred just because my skin is a different color from theirs. Black people as well as white.

"And I didn't help much, because I was ready to defend myself or start a fight even before they said anything. You know, it took me a lot longer than it should have to accept Christ, because I knew Christians were supposed to forgive their enemies and love everybody, and I didn't want to. But you know what? Once I finally gave in and admitted I had a problem and asked Jesus to come into my heart and make me a new person, I discovered that I had the strength to do what was right! Not that it was easy, Shane. It still isn't easy to have people treat me like I'm not as good as them just because of my skin color. But with God's help, I can forgive them. And you know what? When I forgive them, it helps me! All that anger I used to feel was harder on me than it was on them!

"So what should you do? Try to ignore what they say. And pray that God will change them. Because you can't. Only God can change somebody's heart."

"So I should just take it?"

"And pray. Why don't we pray about it right now?" Alicia promptly sat down, shut her eyes, and began talking as if God were right there in the room, asking him to show me how to act and to keep me from doing anything wrong, and praying that I would be able to show others the way to God by my own life.

When she finished, I said, "That's a pretty big order."

"Which part?"

"The one about me being an example for others to find God. If people find out I believe in him, they're more likely not to want to have anything to do with him.

"Don't be so hard on yourself. Ernie and I think you're a pretty nice guy. And so does Todd."

I felt my face getting red. I guess I hadn't had many compliments lately.

When I got home half an hour later, Sandy and his friends were gone. Mom was at work, so I went upstairs, took my books off the bed and piled them on the desk, and looked for my Bible.

I found it on the floor near the clothes hamper. Someone had written inside the cover. It wasn't Sandy's writing.

I guess we should give this back to you.
You need all the help you can get.

I grinned. It was true. I did need all the help I could get.

I sat down with the Bible and read for half an hour, marking anything I thought I should remember, and putting question marks beside things I didn't understand. Todd had said he'd go over my questions next time we worked on math.

Then I got out my school books and began to work in earnest to catch up on what I had missed. It was hard work, and I was glad when Mom came home and called, "Sandy?"

"I'm here, Mom," I said as I went down the stairs.

"Oh, Shane. I wonder—could you—would you mind—just carrying in the things from the car? Your dad let me use it today because I had a lot of groceries to pick up."

"Sure," I said, grabbing my jacket before running out to the car. I made a couple of trips carrying in bags. Then I went to put away my jacket and go back upstairs. But as I took the jacket off, I saw that somebody had printed my initials on the label inside the neck. S.R.D. I looked at the place where it was ripped, but the tear had been mended with tiny, nearly invisible, stitches.

I walked slowly back to the kitchen. "Mom?"

"Yes?"

"Did you fix my jacket?"

She looked flustered. "Didn't I do it right?"

"Sure Mom. It's fine. I mean, thanks."

"You're welcome."

I started to go, and then realized I was capable of putting most of the food away, so I did. Finally, I set the table without being asked.

Supper was quiet. Afterwards, Sandy said he had a date and went out. I wandered around the living room, then decided I may as well hit the books some more.

I was in my room trying to make sense of the Korean War when Dad called me, "Phone, Shane. Some girl."

It was Janice.

"I thought Friday night was when the guy took the girl out? Or is that just on TV?"

"Maybe that's just when the guy has some money."

"We could go for a drive. That doesn't cost anything."

"I take it you don't put the gas in your dad's car."

"Dope. I thought you had your car back now."

"I do, only it doesn't know how to run on water."

"If that's really the problem, I'll fill it up for you—just this once."

"No way."

"Ooh, Macho Man returns."

"Cut it out."

"Are you telling me you'd rather stay home alone on a Friday night than go out with me, even if I have to put gas in your silly car? Or are you really staying home alone? Should I be jealous?"

"No."

"No, what?"

"No, you don't need to be jealous. I was going to study."

"Just one second while I pick myself up off the floor. Is my hearing going? Did Shane Donahue really just tell me that he was going to stay home on a Friday night and study? Is the world about to end?"

"Shut up," I said, but I was smiling.

"Something important must have happened," she insisted. "What have I missed?"

"Look, do you want to go out or not?"

"I asked you first."

"Well, I give up. I'll be over in a few minutes. But I wasn't joking about gas money."

"Neither was I. I'll bring my wallet with me."

Fifteen minutes later, I opened the door to the garage.

The car was cold, and I thought for a minute it wasn't going to start. But after I'd fiddled around a bit, I got it going. I sat there for a few minutes, letting the motor warm up, remembering how excited Sandy and I had been when we'd bought the car three months before we were old enough to get our licenses. We had worked hard on the car, a red Chevy, fixing it up so it would run reasonably well, spending every spare dime we could find to keep it in good shape. And we'd been so proud when we'd at last driven it around the block. But last summer, I had bought Sandy's half of the car. He wanted to save his money for college, and it seemed we just didn't go to the same places any more. He usually got rides from his friends or took the bus.

When I reached Janice's house, I parked the car in front. She didn't come out, so I walked up and rang the bell.

A heavyset, balding man answered the door. He was wearing a pair of good pants and an undershirt, braces dangling at the sides. There was a beer can in his left hand.

"You Shane?" the man asked gruffly.

12

"Yeah," I replied. Then quickly added, "Yes, sir."

"Come on in."

I followed him into the house and sat down in the chair he pointed to.

"She'll be ready in a minute," he said. "Women!"

I didn't know what to say.

"You got any sisters?"

"No.... Sir."

"Lucky," was the man's cryptic comment.

We sat in silence for a minute. Then I ventured a question. "Are you Janice's dad?"

"I don't look like her mother, do I?"

"Uh, no."

He laughed, and I remembered the poem about Santa's belly jiggling like a bowl of jelly.

"Want a soft drink?" he asked. "I'm gonna have another beer, but you wouldn't want that, would you? Not when you're planning on going out with my little girl, huh?"

"Uh, no, thanks."

"Smart boy." He heaved himself out of his chair and left the room. A minute or two later he returned with a fresh can in one hand and a bag of chips in the other and sank back down into the worn cushions.

I was relieved to hear Janice's voice nearby. She was yelling at someone to get a life of his own and leave her alone. As she came into the room, I stood up.

"You here already, Shane? Dad, I need some money."

"What for? You're going on a date, aren't you? Let him pay."

"Da—ad."

"Jan—ice," he mimicked.

"I need some money, Dad."

"I work all week long just to make money for you to spend on some good-looking guy, huh?"

She held out her hand and stuck her tongue out at him.

He laughed, shifted so he could reach into his back pocket, and pulled out a fat wallet. As he opened it and pulled out a wad of bills, he said, "So how much do you need? Fifty? A hundred? You want to break me?"

"Thirty would be fine."

"Here. Take forty. But don't blow it all in one place. And make sure he's worth it."

"Da—ad."

"Sweetie-pie."

"You're horrible," she said as she took the money, then leaned over to kiss his forehead.

"Hey, kid!" he yelled as we walked to the door.

I turned to look at him.

"You take care of her, huh? Only got one daughter. So you better take care of her if you want to stay in one piece!"

"Yes, sir."

"Come on," Janice insisted, pulling me toward the door and outside. We walked to the car and I opened the door for her. Then I got in behind the wheel.

"So now everything's wonderful, huh? Mr. Macho is at the wheel where he belongs!"

I said, "Cut it," but then I laughed.

"Yes, sir," she said meekly.

"Where do you want to go?"

"There's a party at Scott Trenchuk's. We could go there."

"I wasn't invited."

"I thought Scott was a friend of yours?" she asked in surprise.

"I think the operative word is 'was'."

"Well, he invited me," she countered.

"Fine." I turned the car in the direction of Scott's house. The last time I'd been at a party at Scott's was the night Marietta dumped me for Keith, and it was more than likely they would be there tonight. But meeting them wasn't the only reason I didn't want to go. It just didn't seem like much of a place to take God.

There'd be loud music, plenty to drink, and drugs. And there'd be couples sneaking off to be alone. I wondered if Janice had any idea what she was getting into.

Well, I had to face all of them sometime. Why not tonight? And Janice might as well learn a bit more about life.

There were a lot of cars, so I parked down the street from the house. When I opened the door for Janice, she jumped out.

"Let's go," she said happily. "You know the night I picked you up?"

"Yeah."

"Well, I had driven past here a couple of times, trying to get my nerve up to go in alone. I still can't believe I found you outside like that."

"Yeah," I said. "Real great."

I grabbed her hand and she had to run to keep up with my long strides.

No one ever knocked. I pushed the door open and we went in. The music was loud and the air was already filled with smoke. A few couples were dancing in the living room. Others were spread around in small groups drinking and talking, shouting above the music.

I added my own and Janice's coats to the pile in the front hallway. Then I led her into the living room.

"Want to dance?" I asked.

She nodded, and I put my arms around her. Like Marietta's, her head barely came to my shoulder. And like Marietta, she didn't seem to mind my holding her close. But as I held her and we moved slowly, my mind drifted. I was thinking about Ted, who never missed a party. Where was Ted tonight?

Janice's hand touched my cheek, and when I bent down she shouted into my ear, "What are you thinking about?" Before I could reply, she kissed me.

The music stopped, but neither of us realized it. Janice pressed against me, inviting me to keep kissing her. My brain reeled. Maybe she did know what Scott's parties were like, after all.

I felt a hand, warm and strong, on my shoulder. "Well, if it isn't our boy, Shane." It was Keith's voice.

I pushed Janice away and stepped back to face him.

118

His broken nose had healed, and it did look straighter than before. Maybe I should send him a bill for cosmetic surgery.

Marietta was with him, her blond hair silky, golden earrings dangling down to almost touch her bare shoulders, tight black dress hugging the curves until it ended high above her knees, one spiked heel impatiently tapping the floor. She had driven one of those heels into my foot once when she was angry with me. Now, she stood there studying Janice, her blue eyes flashing under the thick black mascara.

Janice's arm crept possessively around my waist.

I glanced down at her, and caught her face alight with excitement.

Keith held out his hand. "No hard feelings, huh? All's fair in love and war."

"Yeah, sure," I said.

"Anyway, you look like you're doing okay." He nodded toward Janice. "I don't think we've met, honey."

"You want something?" I asked.

"No, no," laughed Keith. "I'm not going to steal another girl from you." His dark eyes gleamed with laughter and something else. "Anyway, I'm happy with the one I've got." He put his arm around Marietta's neck and pulled her against him. "Eh, babe?"

Her eyes held mine, and I knew she was daring me to make trouble. But I merely looked back at Keith.

"Hey, come on out to the kitchen, Shane." Keith, with Marietta beside him, moved off and I followed reluctantly. Janice gripped my arm, her eyes shining.

"Here, have a beer." Keith reached inside the fridge and tossed a can to me.

From habit, I caught it, and then I saw Keith offering one to Janice. As she reached her hand out, I grabbed it first. "No way," I said firmly. "Your dad said I was supposed to take care of you."

"Shane Donahue, I am not a baby!"

"Well, you're too young for this."

"You're out of your mind!"

"No!"

"I'm supposed to watch you drink, but I can't?" she asked angrily.

"I'm not going to have one, either." I set both cans on the table.

"Shane, honey, what's the matter with you?" Marietta asked. "I don't remember your ever caring what I drank." There was a barb in her voice.

"That's okay," Keith said. "Shane doesn't have to drink if he doesn't want to. Of course, I did hear some rumors, Shane. You might want to do something to prove they were wrong."

"Rumors?" I asked, but I knew what was coming.

"Yeah, something.... Now what was it again? Something about you chickening out? But, hey, now that I've seen this little number, I don't blame you for not wanting to leave here. But, you know, there was something else. What was it, now? Oh, yeah, something about how you found God. That's it! You found God and now you think you're too good for us. That's what I heard. But, hey, man, you're here now, so it looks like that was wrong, too. So, no problem.

"Oh, that reminds me. I've got something for you. Something you'll like. You and the little girl here can have it. No cost."

He reached into his pocket and then held his hand out.

There was white powder in it.

"What is it, Shane?" Janice asked eagerly.

"Nothing you need to know about."

"Go on, Shane. Take it. You're still one of us, aren't you?" Keith's face leered at me.

"Let's, Shane," Janice said. "You have before, haven't you?"

"What I've done doesn't matter. We're not doing it now."

"Think you're too good for us, now, eh, Shane?" Marietta's voice was hard.

"Didn't you know?" said Keith innocently. "Blondie's got religion, now. He's taken to reading his Bible and talking about God."

Scott's voice came from behind me. "You gonna pray for us, Shane? I guess you're gonna have to pray that we all quit our wicked ways."

A female voice screeched, "Shame on you, Shane, bringing a sweet young thing into this house of sin!"

The taunts continued, and they began to take on a more threatening tone. I kept my eyes on Keith, who was still laughing. But he was swearing, too, and as I looked into his gleaming eyes, I knew he was on more than beer. And I knew what could happen when a mob gets out of control.

Feeling I was caught in some kind of nightmare, I grasped Janice's arm. I began to back up slowly, taking Janice with me. I felt warm flesh behind, but I didn't stop. A male voice said, "Ouch," but whoever it was gave way. I knew they were still a little afraid of me. But a group doesn't fear the way individuals do, and I knew it wouldn't be long.

Clutching Janice's arm tightly, I continued pushing my way backwards out of the room. Reaching the hallway, I grabbed our jackets from the top of the pile beside the door, and forced her protesting figure through the front door.

"Run!" I yelled. She hesitated, but I still had her arm, so she had to keep up. Behind us, the door opened and people crowded through, swearing and yelling for us to come back.

Frightened now, Janice needed no more urging. But we weren't moving fast enough. Just as we reached the car, Keith and several others caught up.

Throwing Janice head first into the front seat, I tossed the keys in after her and slammed the door shut, at the same time yelling, "Lock the doors!" Before I could turn to face the others, rough hands grabbed me and spun me around. I struggled, but Keith and Scott forced me back against the car door. Now what should I do? What had Alicia said about not fighting?

"You used to be one of us, Blondie," Keith said. "Now what are you?"

"What makes you think I've changed?"

"Gone yellow is what I hear."

"I haven't."

"Why'd you come tonight?"

"I don't know."

"Did you come to tell us about God?"

"Yeah," Scott said, his face inches from mine, his breath reeking with alcohol. "You're weak, Shane. You thought you could be one us, but you were wrong. You're weak, just like your sissy brother."

"Leave Sandy out of this!"

"Oh, right. I'm sorry to say anything nasty about your wonderful, stuck-up brother. Know what I think of your brother?" Scott let out a stream of obscenities. I continued my struggle to get free, but there were too many arms holding me against the side of the car.

"Let me go, Keith! I won't come back."

"Yeah? Well, we want to make it clear to you that you aren't invited back, Blondie."

"It's clear already."

"Not as clear as it's going to be!"

"Keith..." I twisted with all my strength, but it was no use. "Keith, don't—"

I saw his fist coming, so I ducked my head. His fist smashed into the metal of the car. Now he was really mad. Someone—I think it was Rory, Marietta's former boyfriend, climbed up on the roof behind me and grabbed a handful of my hair, pulling my head back. This time, Keith didn't miss. Then Scott hit me and a girl screamed. Keith hit me again and again. I tried to kick, but they were holding my legs, too.

As I cried inside for God to help me, a vicious punch found my stomach, and a wave of nausea swept everything else from my mind. A second blow to my ribs made me moan in pain. The hands holding my hair pulled hard as a blow caught me above the right eye. Then another and another. I felt groggy, and was only vaguely aware of police sirens and a girl screaming. Then the ones holding me let go and I dropped heavily to the ground and lay there.

Through a mist of pain, I heard the siren come close and stop, and I heard Janice yelling something about my being hurt. Then she was lifting my head onto her lap and somebody was holding my arm to take my pulse. When I opened my eyes, I saw that there was a lot of blood around. Mine, of course. Mostly from my nose, which was bleeding but good.

I tried to get up, but the cop told me to stay put and ran back to the cruiser.

"Are you okay?" Janice asked. She sounded frightened.

"Yeah, I'm fine," I mumbled through thick lips.

"Wow! Are your friends always like this?"

"Yeah."

"Wow!"

The policeman returned and pressed a pad against the bridge of my nose. "I called an ambulance. What happened?"

"Nothing," I mumbled.

"Look, kid, you're just lucky I was in the neighborhood when somebody called in to say a gang of kids was chasing somebody. Looking at you, I'd say they caught up. So you tell me who they were."

"It isn't what you think."

"Yeah? You figure you earned it or something? Maybe it was an initiation?"

"I don't want to talk about it."

"How about you, young lady? You want to talk about it?"

"I didn't see a thing," Janice replied sweetly, her eyes wide.

"You kids drive me crazy!"

The sound of an ambulance came from down the street.

"This your car?" the policeman asked.

"Yeah."

"I'll drive it," Janice said.

"That okay with you, kid?"

"Yeah, sure." I shut my eyes. My head felt like it was going to burst, and I felt sick. Why couldn't they just leave me alone? Why did they have to keep asking questions?

Strong hands lifted me onto a stretcher. I relaxed and let myself drift off.

I came to on a hospital bed with a nurse washing my face.

"Where am I?" I asked as I struggled to push away her hand.

"Take it easy, buddy. The doctor's coming to look at you and we have to clean you off so he can see."

I sank back and she finished washing off the blood. "How are you feeling?" she asked.

"I'm okay."

"Sure. You guys are always okay."

"What do you mean by that?"

"You know what I mean." She walked out of the room.

I lay there, thinking about what had happened and wondering why God had allowed Keith and the others to beat me up. Why hadn't he protected me? Another ten seconds and I'd have been in the car and gone. What good was my being beaten up? So far as I could see, God didn't seem to be too concerned about what happened to Shane Donahue.

Somebody came and took me for X-rays.

Some time later, a tall, bored-looking young doctor came in and examined me. He put stitches into two cuts on my face.

"Your nose isn't broken, but it's badly bruised. You've got a couple of bruised ribs and your abdomen will be sore, but there's no internal damage. No fractures. You'll live. But maybe you should choose your friends more carefully."

I put my shirt back on. There was blood all over it, but it was all I had to wear home.

"I should probably keep you in overnight for observation. You could have a concussion."

"I'm fine," I said. "I'm going home."

"Do you have someone to drive you?"

"Yeah. I'll be fine."

"Well, I suppose it'll be okay. I'll give you a sheet on concussions, just in case."

The doctor handed me a piece of paper and I walked out. Janice was sitting in the waiting room.

"Have you got my jacket?" I asked after I assured her I was okay.

"No. Mine was on the ground about fifteen feet from the car. But there was no sign of yours. I went most of the way back to Scott's looking for it."

"I guess I dropped it. Oh, man, now I don't have a jacket!"

"I'll get the car warmed up and then come in to get you."

So I sat waiting until she came back about five minutes later. When I stood up, the floor started moving just a little, so I leaned against her as we walked out.

She put me into the passenger side and took the wheel.

"Want to go home?" she asked.

"What time is it?"

"A quarter to twelve."

"Drive around for a few minutes. I need my head to clear."

I slumped back, leaning against the cushions, closing my eyes to the flood of light along the hospital driveway.

How was I going to explain this to my parents?

"I thought those people were your friends," she said after we'd been driving for a while.

"So did I."

"She was your girl, wasn't she?"

"Who?"

"You know who. Marietta."

"Yeah, I guess."

"What happened?"

"She decided I wasn't fun any more. Said I was thinking too much. She decided Keith was more to her liking. That was a long time ago."

"Yeah, at least a couple of weeks."

"Seems like forever."

"So why did they beat you up?"

"Since when do they need a reason?"

She laughed. "Well, knowing you has certainly put more excitement into my life."

"Is that what you wanted?"

She ignored my question and asked a few of her own. "What was all that stuff about religion? What did they mean? Why were they calling you names and everything? What did they mean about you talking about God?"

Oh, no. Now was not the time to tell Janice about my new faith in Christ. God, I prayed silently, whose side are you on, anyway? Where are you tonight? Busy?

"I'd rather tell you about that another time," I said aloud. "Look, I think I'd better go home. I'll get somebody to drive you to your house."

She shrugged. "Okay. If you don't want to tell me, I can't make you."

We drove in silence for a few blocks.

"He's sure strong, isn't he?"

"Who?"

"Keith."

"Yeah, I guess. But he had a lot of help."

"Could you beat him if it was just you and him?"

"If I had to."

"How about Scott?"

"I think so. Never tried."

"Could Sandy beat Keith?"

"Probably."

"But he couldn't beat you, right?" she asked in surprise.

"He has lots of times."

"But I thought you were the tough one!"

"Sandy's more flexible. Also stronger. He'd usually beat me in a fair fight."

"Do you fight dirty?"

"I have."

"I'd like to see you."

At this, I opened my eyes as wide as I could and stared at her. "You'd like to what?"

"I'd like to see you fight Scott and Keith. Dirty. Teach them all a lesson."

"Yeah, right." I shut my eyes again.

We had reached my house. I fumbled with the door handle, and Janice came around to help me out. I leaned against her and she reached up to kiss one of the few places on my face that wasn't cut or bruised. I held her close for a minute, then leaned on her as we went up to the house.

The house was dark and I remembered Mom and Dad had said something about going next door to play bridge. They often played until one.

"Look," I said as she unlocked the door for me, "why don't you take my car home and I'll pick it up tomorrow?"

"Isn't anybody home?" she asked as she swung the door open and turned on the light in the dark hallway.

"No, not yet."

"Well," she said as she began to unbutton my shirt, "in that case I should look after you, shouldn't I?"

13

"There's blood all over your shirt," she said matter-of-factly. "Where's your laundry room?"

"In the basement."

I stood still while she finished unbuttoning my shirt and then took it off. While I waited for her to take it to the basement, I leaned against the wall. I felt worse than I had the morning I'd been hung over.

After what seemed like forever, she returned. "Where's your room?"

I jerked my head toward the stairs and she draped my arm around her shoulder so she could help me walk. I think it probably would have been less painful to crawl up the stairs by myself, but I didn't know how to say so.

We got to the room at last, and I carefully collapsed on my bed. I just wanted to lie there on my back and pass out. But Janice didn't leave.

"Is this Sandy's room, too?" she asked in surprise. She picked up an old teddy bear from a shelf above Sandy's desk.

"Don't touch that!"

"I'm not going to hurt it." She pouted. "Besides, what does it matter to you?"

"Just don't touch his stuff!"

"You'd think I was going to contaminate it," she said, but she put it down and came over to stand above me.

"Is it okay if I touch what belongs to you?" she asked sweetly. Then she bent forward, letting her hands move along my arms and slip around my shoulders. Her lips touched my cheek as she pressed against me.

"Don't, Janice," I mumbled. "Not now."

But she kept kissing me, all the time talking softly about how brave I was and how she liked being around me.

"Stop it!" I said with as much force as I could manage.

She got up as if stung. "Boy, you're a lot of fun, aren't you? I just wanted to make you feel better. Isn't that what Marietta would have done?"

I didn't answer.

"What's this?"

I turned to see what she was talking about and then shut my eyes. She had picked up my Bible and she was reading the inscription Paul or Wilf had written in it.

"I don't get it," she said in a puzzled voice. "Why have you got a Bible?"

It was so hard to talk, but I had to say something, "Because.... I'm a Christian now. Since last Friday night."

"A Christian? I don't get it."

"It means—it means I believe in God. I asked him to take over my life. I've been making a big mess of it on my own."

Light dawned. "That's what Keith and Scott were talking about! I don't believe it! Shane Donahue! Here I am thinking I finally found a guy who's a real man! I wanted to be just like you and do the things you did...you and Keith and Ted and Marietta and the rest. I wanted you to be the first guy I really loved.... And you pick now to go soft! I can't believe it!"

"That's not true," I said with an effort.

"What isn't true?"

"I—I don't know. My head—I can't think.... Just that it isn't like it seems. Even Ted.... It isn't any fun."

"You want fun? I'll show you fun!" She pressed her hands hard against my ribs. Pain swallowed me up and everything went black.

The first thing I was conscious of was Mom's voice calling my name.

I opened my eyes and yelled, "Yeah?" But the word was muffled by my swollen lips.

Now she was in the doorway, and her voice sounded worried. "Shane, wake up!"

"Yeah?" I answered, struggling to sit. I hurt everywhere.

"Shane! What happened?"

"Nothing. I'm okay."

"What on earth's going on?" Sandy complained from the other bed.

"The police want to see Shane."

"What else is new!" he grumbled as he turned onto his stomach with his pillow over his head.

"Police?" I repeated.

"They're downstairs. Your dad said to get you. Oh, Shane, what's wrong? Why do you have those bandages on your face? And those bruises? What kind of trouble are you in? What's that paper all over you? Shane, what—?"

"It's nothing, Mom. Honest. Go on down. I'll be there in a minute." As she hesitated, I repeated. "Go on. It's okay."

"It doesn't look okay. And the police...." But she turned and went slowly back down the stairs.

I brushed papers onto the floor and struggled to get out of bed. What were the papers? I picked one up and stared at it, but the words made no sense. Then I saw the ruined cover and realized what it was. "Did you do this?" I asked Sandy.

He turned over. "Did I do what?"

"Somebody wrecked my Bible."

"Well, I didn't do it."

"Was it like this when you came in?"

"How should I know? I got in after one and you were asleep, so I never turned on the light."

He watched me drag myself out of the bed.

"What did happen?" he asked.

"Nothing. I'm okay."

"I just asked. I didn't say I cared!" He buried his head under his pillow again.

I still had my pants on, so I found a shirt, thrust my feet into an old pair of moccasins, and went to the bathroom. I was a mess. Besides the two cuts where the doctor had put stitches, my nose and lips were swollen, and my left eye was partly closed. And if that wasn't enough, I needed to shave. But how?

I decided that combing my hair was all I could manage, so I did that and then painfully descended the stairs. Mom and Dad were in the hallway with two cops, one a lady.

"You Shane?" the male cop asked.

"Yeah, I'm Shane."

"Looks like you lost an argument with a wildcat. Or should I ask how the other guy looks?"

"Are you here about that?"

"Should we be?"

"No. I just thought.... Why are you here?"

"We have a few questions we want to ask you."

"What kind of questions?"

"Why don't we sit down?" the female cop said. "You look like you need to."

I led the way into the living room and sank cautiously into a chair. Mom and Dad followed the cops and stood in the doorway.

"You're eighteen, right?" the female cop asked.

"Yeah. My birthday was last month."

"We'd like to talk to Shane alone for a moment, if you don't mind." The female cop was looking at Mom and Dad. "We have a missing persons report on Ted Cummings and we're talking to some of his friends."

Mom's body visibly jerked, and the look of relief in her eyes sent a strange feeling through me. She was terrified that I was in trouble.

Dad reluctantly followed her into the kitchen.

"You look like you got worked over pretty good. How come you didn't fight back?" asked the female officer.

I stared at her in surprise. "How—?"

"Your knuckles aren't bruised," she answered.

"Oh? Yeah." I looked down at my hands. They were smooth and clean. No trace even of the fight I'd had with Keith two weeks before.

"Something we should look into?" the male officer asked.

"No," I said. "Some guys held me while some others beat me up. A cop was called and he called for an ambulance."

"Anything to do with Ted's disappearance?"

"No."

"What, then?"

"Nothing important."

"You he-men types really get to me," the lady cop said. "Somebody beats you up and you put on this big 'I'm okay. I can take it.' act."

The nurse last night had said something similar. This time I saw red. "All right. You want to know about it? Some of my so-called friends beat me up because they found out I'd started going to church and reading a Bible!"

The officers stared at me.

"Are you putting us on?" the woman said.

"No."

"Well, that isn't exactly the impression we had been given of you."

"I know. I—I've changed." I looked down at the floor, embarrassed by what I'd revealed.

"In case you're interested," she said, "I also go to church and I read my Bible every day."

I stared at her in surprise.

"There are a few of us around, you know," she smiled.

"What about Ted?" the other officer asked impatiently. "His dad came down to the station yesterday and said he'd been gone since Sunday. The teachers at the school say they haven't seen him since a week ago Wednesday. We've talked to a few kids, and they told us to talk to you. We were here last evening, but nobody was home. You know anything?"

"I don't know—" I began, but the officer interrupted.

"Look, we've already heard that he was talking about running away and that you were thinking of going with him. So save any lies you plan to tell."

"I wasn't going to lie," I said with as much dignity as I could muster under the circumstances. "I was going to say that I don't know where he is but that he talked about going downtown and I assume that's what he did."

"Why?"

"Because he was sick of going to school, and having a hard time with his dad because he was failing, and he thought he could manage his life better on his own."

"Could he have gone to live with his mother?"

"His mom left a few years ago."

"Does he know where she is?"

"I don't think so. She just left a note one day saying she'd gone away with somebody and she wouldn't be back. Ted figured the guy she went with didn't want a kid along."

"Sounds rough," the woman officer said.

"Yeah."

"So he wouldn't have gone to her?" the man said.

"He's never mentioned her to me."

"How was he planning on living? Did he have money?"

"He said there were lots of ways to get money."

"Sure there are. He on drugs?"

"I don't—well, he's tried some. Not hard stuff. And not much. Mostly, he just drinks beer."

"He have a girl friend who might know something?"

"No. He didn't have much good to say about women. Because of his mom, I guess."

"All right." The male officer shut his notebook and stood up.

The female officer stood, too, so I pulled myself out of the chair. She winked at me. "Hang in there, huh?"

"Yeah," I said.

"And put on the full armor."

Not having a clue what she was talking about, I let that pass. I walked to the door with them and shut it after they had gone out.

"What was that all about?" Dad had come up behind me.

"They wanted to know if I knew where Ted has gone."

"And do you?"

"Not really. I told them everything I know."

"They weren't here about you?"

"No."

"Who were you fighting with?"

"Nobody." I saw Dad getting ready to yell, and quickly said, "I wasn't fighting. I got beat up, but I didn't fight."

"And just why didn't you?"

"I—uh—"

"I suppose you just stood there and let them hit you! That's what happens when you start going to church. Sissy stuff! Don't you ever do anything so stupid again! Next time somebody tries to hit you, you stand up like a man and fight, or you don't bother coming home!" Dad turned and walked into the living room, picked up the morning newspaper he had been reading when the cops arrived, and buried himself in the sports section.

I stood there like I was rooted. Mom was watching me, her eyes concerned. But my dopey sense of humor, absent for the last couple of months, chose this moment to emerge. I had to go as fast as I could to the kitchen and bury my face in a towel.

Laughing hurt both my chest and stomach incredibly, but how could I help it? Here was my dad upset, not because I'd been beaten up, but because I hadn't fought back!

I felt something touch my shaking back. Startled, I looked around to see Mom's worried face.

When she realized I was laughing, she quickly drew her hand back.

"It's okay, Mom," I choked out. "I'm sorry, but it was funny."

Her brow puzzled, she set about making an eggnog and finding a straw so I could drink it.

Sandy came in as I was finishing the drink. "I saw the cops leave," he said. "So what happened?"

"Nothing," I said.

"Yeah, sure. What did they come here for?"

"They were looking for Ted. They heard I was his friend."

"They weren't here about you?"

"No."

"Where'd you go last night?"

"Nowhere."

"All right, don't tell me. I'll hear fast enough."

"I'm sure you will."

"What's that supposed to mean?"

"Nothing," I said wearily as I started out of the room.

"All I can say," Sandy called to my back, "is I'd like to shake hands with whoever did it. You've had it coming for a long time."

"Sandy!" Mom exclaimed in horror.

"Well, he has."

I went upstairs, trying to block Sandy's words out of my mind. The pieces of my Bible were scattered all over my bed and floor. The last thing I remembered was that Janice had been mad at me. She must have torn up the Bible after I passed out.

I picked up some of the pieces and then sank onto my bed. What did it matter, anyway? God seemed so far away. I'd thought things would get better after I gave my life to him, but things weren't any better. Those who had been my friends hated me; Janice was furious with me; Sandy and my dad loathed me; Ted had really gone and no one knew where he was; and soon I'd be the laughing stock of the whole school.

They'd all hear how I'd become a Christian and they'd expect me to act differently, only I still seemed to mess up everything. So what good was it?

And Dad had said I couldn't go to church, so how was I supposed to learn more about God or about how to act?

I threw the pieces of paper I was holding into my wastebasket. It was just a book, anyway. How could a book help me?

Painful as it would be, I decided to have a shower. When I came back to my room, I found Ernie waiting.

"Hi," I said. "Come to stare?"

"What on earth happened to you?"

"Can you believe I'm already tired of that question?"

"Keith?"

"Good guess. You win the lottery. How did you know?"

"Lucky guess. I heard Keith and Scott talking about how you'd said something to Ted about God."

I sat down on the bed to put my socks on. It hurt like blazes to bend over, and finally Ernie took over.

"You work today?" I asked as he finished.

"Not until four. I thought we could do something, but from the looks of you..."

"I look worse than I am. Do you think Todd's around?"

"Yeah, he's coming to our place for lunch. He and Alicia have a bunch of wedding junk to do—choosing invitations and stuff like that."

"Think he'd have a minute to spare?"

"Sure. Got a problem? I mean, other than the obvious?"

"Yeah. I thought God was going to help me start over and everything. So far, all he's done is make everything worse. And my dad says I can't go to church."

"Why would he say that?"

"Search me. Something about standing on my own two feet and not needing a crutch. He even thought I got beat up because I went to church."

"Didn't you?"

I looked at him in surprise. "Yeah, I guess maybe in a way I did. Only that's not quite what he meant."

"Not to change the subject, but did you hear the cops are looking for Ted?"

"Yeah. They talked to me."

"Figured so. You were likely his best friend."

"I wasn't much of a friend."

"What do you mean?"

"I realized a few days ago that I never really cared about him. He was just somebody I did things with. A friend should be more than that."

"Yeah, I guess. We've got a lot to learn."

"I have. You've been a friend to me."

Ernie looked away in embarrassment. "I didn't do anything."

"You made me go with you last Friday night. If you hadn't, who knows where I'd be right now. Maybe dead."

We didn't talk as Ernie put my shoes on and I picked up my wallet.

When I was ready, I said, "My car's over at Janice's. Can you give me a ride there?"

"Sure, let's go."

I remembered that my jacket had disappeared, so I hunted around and found an old one.

We drove over to Janice's. I was tempted to let Ernie get my keys for me. But then I decided I needed to talk to her. Painfully, I got out of the car and walked up to ring the door bell. A boy about ten came to the door, disappeared, and returned with Janice.

"Well, aren't you good-looking!" she said scornfully.

"Janice, we need to talk."

"What about?"

"You know. Last night."

"About how you got beat up?"

"No. You know what about."

"Oh, you mean how I thought you were the kind of guy I wanted?"

"Yeah, that."

"Well, anyone can make a mistake."

"Look, you've got it all wrong. You—"

"No, you've got it wrong. The next time I go to one of Scott's parties, I'll go with Scott, or maybe Keith, not a wimp like you."

"The parties aren't worth it. You don't want to get caught up in all that stuff."

"Look, Shane, you run your life and I'll run mine."

"Your dad wouldn't like it," I was grasping at straws and I knew it.

Her voice grated, "My father? You mean the beer guzzler who's nothing but bluff and bluster? The one who likes nothing better than to hang around in nightclubs with blondes like your friend Marietta on his arm? I should care what he likes?"

"You seemed to care that he didn't want anybody else driving his car."

"Why should I let you drive? I'm every bit as capable as you." Her voice was mocking. "And you were such a gentleman, weren't you? I should have realized you were nothing but a phony." She threw my car keys past me onto the sidewalk, yelled, "Creep!" and then slammed the door.

The sickness I felt had nothing to do with being hit last night. How do you keep another person from messing up her life? Despite what had happened, I still thought Janice was a nice kid. Only it looked like she was just as mixed up as I had been.

Ernie came and picked up the keys for me.

"I heard her yell something about you're being a creep," he said cheerfully as he handed me the keys. "She mad because you got beat up?"

"Not really. She's another one who doesn't like the idea of my going to church."

"You could make a list."

"Yeah, maybe I will."

We drove both cars to Ernie's house. Todd was already there. When he saw me, he came out with the inevitable question.

"I'm okay," I said. "This is all part of the great job God's doing taking care of me."

14

Todd began to laugh.

"Yeah, it sure is funny," I said.

"Sorry, but you were trying to be funny, weren't you?"

"Not particularly. I thought God was going to take care of me, so I guess this is part of it."

"You're blaming God because you got in a fight?"

Patiently, I explained to Todd what had happened, including my dad's telling me not to go to church.

"So now what do I do?" I asked.

"What did that policewoman say again?"

"Something about putting on the full armor. Whatever that means."

"Ephesians 6," said Todd. "That means that you're like a soldier, only you need special armor—truth, righteousness, peace, faith, salvation, and the Bible as your sword."

"Do you really think this is all God's plan for his life?" Ernie asked.

"Could be," Todd replied. "Why not? The early Christians didn't exactly have it easy. Nearly every one of the disciples and others who were close to Jesus were murdered for their faith in some way or another. So why shouldn't God let Shane have a rough time?"

"Oh, man," I groaned as I sank carefully into a chair.

"You say everything's gone wrong," Todd said, "but what exactly do you mean by that? Okay, so Janice dumped you. Does that greatly affect you?"

"Well, no, I guess not."

"You'd be a lot better off finding a girlfriend who's a Christian. The Bible says not to be closely tied to an unbeliever. So now you're free for God to work in that area. How about Keith and the others? Will you miss being their friend?"

"I guess not."

"And now you have an opportunity to witness to them."

"How?"

"By doing what the Bible says—showing kindness to your enemies. Let God handle the revenge, not you. Kill them with kindness. They'll notice."

"You make it sound so easy. What about my dad?"

"Do what he says. Don't go to church. But I'll bring you tapes of the services. And you pray for him and for your mom. God works through our prayers. Do you think he'll let you keep going to house group?"

"He doesn't seem to mind my going out with Ernie. I just won't tell him about the house group."

"So you think it's okay for you to keep going there?"

"I need to. I don't mind missing the worship service, especially when I can listen to the tape. But I'd really miss house group. I need to be there."

"What if he asks you if it's connected with the church?"

"I don't think he will. If he does.... Well, I won't lie."

"Okay. So—anything else?"

"What about the whole school laughing at me?"

"Let it. Don't react. Just go about your business. The kids will notice there's something different about you."

"Yeah, they'll think I've turned into some kind of zombie."

"I don't think so."

"I sure hope you know what you're talking about."

"The thing is, Shane, when we accept Christ, we immediately get tested to see how solid our faith is. Not by God, but by Satan. You see, Satan is God's enemy, and when we become God's children, we get his enemy for our enemy.

"It's Satan who wants to get us derailed. If we're reading our Bibles, he wants to get us confused so we'll stop. If we're praying, he wants to get us frustrated. If we're trying to lose bad habits, he tries to make us think we can't give them up. And what we have to do is cling even tighter to God. That way, when we come through, our faith will be that much stronger for the next time."

"That's just what's happened! I didn't think it was worth reading the Bible any more. I didn't see how it could help."

"Now, tell me, what's happened that's good?"

"Not much."

"Anything?"

"Well, my phys ed teacher said he'd give me some coaching in running even though I'm not able to be on the track team."

"What else?"

"I guess my mom and I are getting along better. I think she—I think she really does care what happens to me."

"Great. What else?"

"Well, maybe the one police officer's being a Christian. That likely helped."

"Right. Keep going."

"Thanks to you, I'm starting to understand math. And I'm working on my school....You're right! Everything isn't bad."

"It never is. Only, too often we're looking for big things when God is working through little ones."

"And now that you've finished your sermon," said Alicia, "we have some little things to take care of ourselves. Not wanting to chase you two away, but this gentleman and I have a wedding to organize."

"Go to it," Ernie said. "We'll be upstairs if you need advice."

I followed Ernie up to his room and lay down on his bed with my head on a couple of pillows.

"Feel better?" he asked as he pulled out a chair and straddled it.

"Some. But I guess I need to get a new Bible."

"How come?"

"Janice trashed mine last night."

"Nice of her."

"Yeah."

"Alicia likely has an extra. I'll go see."

Ernie was back in a few minutes. "Here." He held out a beige Bible. "Alicia says you can keep it. It's one she got from somebody, but she's never used it. She's got a huge one with all kinds of extra stuff in it."

"Thanks." I took the Bible and looked at it. It was much bigger than the one I'd had before because this one had both the

Old and New Testaments in it. I found John and Acts and felt better. I'd just have to do a lot more reading so I could learn what was in all the other books.

"Want to do something?" Ernie asked.

"With this face?"

"Yeah, I can see your point. We could rent a movie?"

"Maybe." I thought for a minute. "No, I think I should work. I've got a lot of catching up to do."

"Want me to help? I've got Bs in a couple of subjects, you know."

"History?"

"Bingo."

"Okay, you can be my history tutor."

So Ernie got some soft drinks, with a straw for me, and found his history books, and we settled down to work.

At five o'clock, I drove home. Nobody was there, so I went up to my room and sat down on the bed. Someone had cleaned up the rest of the torn pages and changed the bedding.

I sat down and picked up my new Bible. I figured I should take the opportunity to read it while I was alone.

I read for a while, and then I found myself talking to God, telling him about everything that had gone wrong and asking him to help me. And I remembered to ask him to look after Ted, wherever he was. Who knew what kind of trouble he was in?

After a while I felt restless, so I went downstairs.

I hadn't heard anybody come in, but Mom was in the kitchen making omelets. I offered to help. She looked at me in surprise.

"Well," she said doubtfully, "I was going to make a salad."

"Okay," I said, opening the refrigerator door and wondering where she kept the lettuce.

Mom found it for me, then got me a knife, bowl, and cutting board.

"You aren't going out tonight, are you?" she asked.

"No."

"Are—are you sure you're okay? You look—well, like you must be in pain."

"It's a bit sore, but I'm okay." I cut a slice of lettuce and wondered what to do with it.

Mom reached over and began tearing the lettuce into the bowl. "Please be careful," she said, her eyes on the lettuce. "You might have been badly hurt."

I started tearing the rest of the lettuce. "Don't worry. It won't happen again."

"Why did they do it, Shane?"

I wondered what to tell her. Finally, I opted for the truth. "A bunch of my old friends found out I'd gone to church and all. They thought I'd turned against them, I guess. So it was like they were teaching me a lesson."

She stopped tearing lettuce and looked intently into my eyes. "Did they?"

I ignored the lettuce, too. "You mean am I going to stop going to church?"

"Yes."

"No."

"But your dad...!"

"I won't go on Sundays if he says I can't. But I won't stop because I got beat up."

"Does—does it mean that much?"

"Not going to church."

I tried to think what to say. Words were hard. I said a silent "Help" to God. "It's not that. It's God. He's giving me a chance to start over. Every stupid thing he—he forgives...and he's there to help me not do so many dumb things in the future. I'll still mess up, but he won't ever give up on me!"

"You really believe there is a God who—who loves us?"

"Yeah, Mom." A rush of confidence came into me. "I don't just believe it; I know it."

"Even after all that's happened to you?"

"Yes."

"What about me, Shane? Do you think I could—what you said—start over?"

"How's supper coming?" Dad asked as he entered the kitchen. "You aren't moving very fast from the looks of it, Elise."

Seeing Mom's frightened look, I quickly went back to tearing lettuce. Dad talked to Mom, acting like I wasn't even there. Inside, my heart was pounding. Mom wanted me to tell her about God—wanted to know if God loved her, too! It was unbelievable! Here I had been thinking God wasn't looking after me, and now my own mother wanted my help!

Afterwards, up in our room, Sandy said, "I hear it was Keith and Scott and your old buddies who got you last night."

"Yeah."

"Janice take good care of you?"

"Sure."

"You have a knack for making people dislike you, huh?"

"Whatever you say."

"What are you trying to prove?"

"Nothing."

"So what's with this Bible act?"

"Nothing."

"Real talkative, aren't you? Think I enjoy having a brother who's the laughingstock of the school?"

"If you're ashamed of me, I'm sorry."

"What's with you, anyway?" Sandy's voice was gaining in volume as he became more and more angry.

"I don't care if you want to yell at me, but don't let Mom hear."

"Oh, yeah, right. Now you're all concerned about bothering Mom. Since when?" But he lowered his voice.

"Does it matter?" I asked wearily.

"It's just that it isn't like you to be concerned about anybody except yourself, that's all."

I looked at him, but no words came to me. I lay down on my back, too sore and exhausted to be angry. I just wanted Sandy to leave me alone.

Sandy changed his clothes and went out with a parting shot. "Enjoy your own company. You seem to be the only person who can stand it."

I lay still. My face was hurting, as were the muscles of my stomach and my lower ribs. But it wasn't physical pain that brought the tears to my eyes.

In a few minutes, however, I was asleep.

I woke up a couple of hours later. The TV was on downstairs. I went to the bathroom and got ready for bed. I sat up, reading an English book that had been assigned long ago. With my marks, I would have to write the final exam, so I figured I may as well get caught up on the reading.

I read for over an hour, and then fell asleep.

Sandy and I both slept till almost noon. Without speaking, we dressed and went downstairs, where Mom was making sandwiches for lunch.

The meal was quiet. Dad talked to Sandy a little—pointed comments guaranteed to show me what he thought of me.

Mom didn't speak unless Dad asked her a question.

I said nothing. In fact, it was almost like I wasn't even there.

After lunch, they sat in the living room, reading the paper or watching TV. I went to my room.

Shortly after one, Sandy called me to the door.

Ernie had stopped by with a tape of the worship service. I put the tape into my pocket and went back upstairs.

A few minutes later Sandy came to the room. "You're actually working on school, huh? You haven't done any work all year. Why start now?"

I felt the old anger surging up. First Dad, now Sandy. Why couldn't they leave me alone? But I didn't get mad, and I didn't say anything.

Sandy kept at me. "I'd just like to know what kind of game you're playing now, that's all!"

"I'm not playing a game, and if you don't believe me that's your problem."

I sat at my desk and opened my math book, resolutely trying to hold back my temper. I remembered Todd's saying no one could make you lose it because you had control. But it was hard.

However, after a couple more attempts to needle me, Sandy left the room and I breathed a sigh of relief. Then I began working on my homework.

An hour later, there was a soft tap on the door.

I looked up in surprise as Mom's face appeared.

"May I come in?" she asked hesitantly.

"Sure."

"Sandy's gone out and your dad's asleep. I thought—if you don't mind—we were talking in the kitchen. Before your dad came in."

I nodded.

"I asked if you thought your—your God—would give me a second chance. You didn't answer me. I mean, you couldn't, because your father came in."

"Yeah, I know. Sure he would, Mom. He'll give it to anybody."

"I don't know much about God. Once, I went to a Bible study with a neighbor. She was really nice. So kind and so—so happy. But your dad found out and made me stop. That was a long time ago. When you and Sandy were babies."

I remembered the tape in my pocket. "I've got a tape of the worship service this morning. Would you like to listen to it with me?"

She looked around nervously. "As long as your dad doesn't wake up and hear us."

"I'll play it low." I put the tape into my tape deck and we both sat and listened. The singing wasn't bad, but the sermon was just what I needed. It was based on Matthew 6, and it talked about how God looks after people. It said that he knew all about every sparrow, so of course he knows about every person. And it talked about his caring even when he seemed far away.

When the tape ended, there were tears in Mom's eyes.

"I've never paid much attention to God, Shane," she said. "How do I start?"

15

My heart was pounding. What should I say? I barely knew anything myself! But as I remembered the rally and what Todd had told me, I calmed down.

"Well," I said slowly, "God came down to earth in the form of a man. That's Jesus Christ. And he died in our place. Only, because he never did anything wrong, God raised him from the dead. And that's why he can give us a new life. So you have to ask God to forgive you for all the wrong things you've done, and ask Jesus to come into your life and take over.

"That's about it, I guess. You have to tell him you want him to take over and make you a new person.

"And then you need to read your Bible and talk to him a lot, even when it looks like he's left you alone. Because he won't, no matter how it seems."

"Just tell him?"

"Yeah."

"I don't have to do anything else?"

"You can't. None of us can be good enough. So we have to let him take over everything."

"Should I just say it, now?"

"Well, we should close our eyes. You know, to pray." I felt a surge of confidence. "I'll pray first, if you want."

"Would you?" she asked in wonder.

"Sure. God, I know you care about us because you say in the Bible you do. And because of Todd and Ernie and Alicia. Help my mom to know it, too."

"Dear God," Mom said slowly, "I know I've made a lot of mistakes in the past. Please forgive me for them. I've done a lot of wrong things, wicked things. I'm sorry. Please change me. Help me to do the right things. Help me—" She began to sob. "Help me with my family. Teach us to love one other. Help all of us to rely on you and not on ourselves. And please—" she whispered, "please take away Walt's anger."

There was silence for a moment. I sat awkwardly, my mind in turmoil.

"Mom," I said finally, "are you okay?"

She raised her eyes to meet mine. There was a light in them I'd never seen before.

"Yes, Shane." She nodded, "I'm okay. I think I've wanted to do that ever since I went to the Bible study I told you about. I've always known, somehow, that it was right. But I never had the courage to do it before. Your father..." her voice drifted away, and then surged like a wave in the ocean. "But you gave me the courage." She leaned forward to kiss my cheek. "Thank you, Shane."

Then she sat back, her hand covering her mouth. After a moment she said, "We mustn't say anything for a while. We must pray for your dad and for Sandy. Now, I'd better go check on the chicken I put in the oven."

"Mom."

"Yes, Shane?"

"I'm sorry I didn't tell you I was fired. There seemed to be so much already. I thought—I thought that might be the last straw."

She nodded. "Yes, I can understand why you wouldn't want to tell us."

"I'm sorry."

"It's okay. It doesn't matter any more."

She got up to leave.

"Mom?"

"Yes, Shane?"

"I've taken money from your purse a few times."

"I know."

"It was wrong. I knew it. I'll pay you back as soon as I can. I'm going to sell the car. And I'll try to get another job."

"Don't worry, Shane. And....I don't think you should tell your father. Not now."

"Okay."

She went out, and I sank back onto the bed. I felt better for having told Mom about taking her money, but mostly I felt as if

I were dreaming. This past hour couldn't have really happened, could it?

My mother? Saying I had given her courage? It was unbelievable. I lay there, thanking God for what he'd done. I remembered the sermon from the Sunday before, and how I'd been skeptical that God could ever use me to do anything for him!"

I lay there for about fifteen minutes. I couldn't remember ever feeling so good except maybe that first moment I'd realized God loved me.

Finally, I remembered I needed to get to work again. I had gone back to studying science when Sandy came in half an hour later.

"So, did you have a fun afternoon studying?" he asked sarcastically.

There was no anger left in me. I looked up at him. "I had a great afternoon!"

"Yeah, right." But Sandy looked puzzled. He sat on his bed. Seeing my science book, he asked, "So what is quantum mechanics?"

"The part of physics that describes the atom and how atomic particles move," I answered, grinning as much as I could with my face the way it was.

Sandy didn't reply. Instead, he got out his math book and began working on an assignment for the next day.

Still grinning, inside at least, I went back to my science and worked on it until Mom called us for supper.

We both continued to work on our schoolwork during the evening, but we didn't speak again. We went to bed the same way.

I was up early the next morning. I felt about as much like running as like walking to the North Pole, but I forced myself to get up and dress quietly, so as not to waken Sandy. I grabbed some cereal and a piece of toast, threw together a peanut butter sandwich for lunch, found an apple, and left for school. It was tempting to take my car, but that seemed stupid when I was going early to run. So I walked.

I had changed to shorts and done a couple of painful stretches when Mr. Anderson came into the gym.

"You beat me," said the coach.

Then he caught sight of my face. The cuts still had stitches in them, the bruises were a livid purple, and I hadn't shaved yet, so my overall appearance was pretty gross. "Who worked you over?" he asked.

"Nobody important," I said as matter-of-factly as I could. "I look worse than I am."

"Okay. If it doesn't bother you, it doesn't bother me. Let's see what you do for warming up."

We began work, with Mr. Anderson pointing out mistakes I was making and giving me things to work on. Then I began running, slowly, was stopped to be given directions, began again, and so on for nearly half an hour. At that point others began coming in.

"Okay, do five laps to cool down and then hit the shower," Mr. Anderson said. "I'll see you in the morning."

I was early for my first class. I figured I was in for a lot of ribbing, but I had decided to get there ahead of everybody else and take it as it came.

But although a lot of kids looked at me in surprise and made comments to each other, no one spoke to me.

I ate lunch with Ernie, saw Marietta and Keith giggling and looking at me, and wondered what on earth I'd ever seen in either of them.

"I must have been out of my skull," I said out loud.

"Huh?" Ernie said.

"Oh, just thinking out loud," I said. Then I inclined my head in their direction and added, "Them. What on earth made me hang around with them?"

"Good question. I always wondered that myself. Not that you'd ever have listened to my advice."

"Was I that bad?"

"You want the truth?"

I nodded.

"Then, yes. Nobody could tell you anything. You were like ice."

"I wonder why."

"I think I know."

"Yeah? Well, Einstein, enlighten me."

"Because of Sandy."

"I don't know what you mean."

"You and Sandy used to be inseparable. Then, the last year or so, he started getting real popular."

"So?"

"So, the way I figure it, you felt left out and you decided to get your own friends. He was with the "in" group, so you chose the "out" group."

"You make me sound like some kind of idiot."

"Nope. Todd says it was perfectly natural."

"Is that where all this came from? Todd?"

"Mostly. I mean, I told him what I knew, and he explained it to me."

"Thanks."

"You asked."

"Did I?"

"Yeah. And I was saying it to help you figure things out."

"Yeah. The dumb thing is when you put it like that it makes sense. Only, now that I'm no longer part of the 'out' group—although most people may not know that yet—what do I do? Just be alone?"

"Don't I count for anything?"

"Sure you do. I didn't mean that the way it sounded."

"Start your own group."

"Huh?"

"The 'in-Christ' group."

I laughed. "How many of us are there?"

"I don't know. Most of the kids from the church, like Brad and the others, seem to go to other schools. There are a few from our school who go to the church, and there must be some who go to other churches, but to the best of my knowledge, there's nobody who's a leader. So the profile is pretty low. It takes somebody like you to get things cooking."

"Did Todd tell you that, too?"

"Yeah."

"Thank him for me, huh?"

"He says you're a leader who just needs a cause. Now you have one."

"So he wants me to take all the flak for being a Christian in the high school?"

"That's not exactly how he put it."

"Yeah, right."

The bell went, and we gathered up our garbage and books and headed for the first afternoon class. I couldn't help the smile that lit my eyes as I thought of what I would tell Todd when I saw him next. Only it occurred to me that most of the words were ones I couldn't very well use now that I was a Christian. Having God with me all the time left a big gap in my vocabulary.

I was still smiling when I went into English class. Mr. McNeely was handing back the short stories we'd had to write, and as I walked to my desk, the smile was erased. I vaguely recalled reading my story to Ted while we were getting drunk. If only I'd known then what I knew now, maybe I could have said something to help him. Or maybe not. Who knew?

The story came plopping down onto the desk as I sat down. I barely glanced at it, expecting to see, at best, a C. More likely a D.

I did a doubletake. An A+ was written at the top of the page. Beside it was the comment, "I always knew you were capable of something like this."

I looked up. McNeely was standing watching me. I looked back at the paper. I could hear the ripple of shock that was going through the class as the news of my mark spread through. I knew what they were saying.

"Shane Donahue?"

"It must be a mistake."

"It must be Sandy's story."

"Maybe he copied it from somewhere."

I got out a book and pretended to read while the rest of the stories were handed out. But my heart was pounding again.

Somehow, I got through that class and the next one, and was glad to see Ernie waiting for me at my locker. I grabbed the books I needed, and we hurried to Ernie's car.

"So," Ernie said as he drove out of the parking lot. "You've created quite a stir. First the way you look, then an A+ in English. Not a bad day."

"Shut up, okay?"

"Next you'll be getting an A in the math test."

"Not a chance."

"I don't know. Todd's put in a lot of work with you."

"Look, I should pass, but that's all."

"Even that will cause people to wonder what's happened."

"Shut up, okay?" I said with an attempt at a smile. "Want to get a milkshake?"

"I'm broke, remember?"

"I'm not."

"I don't like blowing your money."

"Since when?" Ernie asked in surprise.

"Since—oh, you know when."

"You really have changed, haven't you?" His surprise was genuine.

"Haven't you?" I asked, puzzled.

"Not a whole lot. I was dull and ordinary before, and I still am."

"Maybe you just didn't need to change as much as I do. You hadn't messed up everything the way I had."

"I don't know. Sometimes I wish I had."

"No way."

"I guess." There was a pause. "Anyway, I don't mind buying you a milkshake. You'd do the same for me. Now," he added.

I laughed.

Ernie drove to a restaurant and we ordered milkshakes and fries.

We ate slowly, talking about football and the people from the house group, and finally I told Ernie about what had happened with Mom.

"Wow," he gasped. "That's—that's incredible! Your mom?"

"Yeah. I think she really meant it, too."

"What did your dad say?"

"He doesn't know. He'll likely blow up."

"What about Sandy?"

"I don't know. We just don't talk at all. Other than to be nasty to each other, I mean. Though I'm trying not to do that any more. I think he's puzzled."

"I know he is. I saw him looking at you in English this morning. Like he couldn't believe it."

"Yeah."

Back home, I found a note to say Mom was at work. From the sound of voices, Sandy was in the basement with Paul or one of his other friends. I went upstairs to work on my homework.

The next few days went by in the same way. I was up early to run. Mr. Anderson was usually around to advise me and spur me to work harder, and sometimes to run with me. As I did my homework, my classes began to make more sense. I got a 73 in math, and 61 in a science quiz. Not wonderful, maybe, but tons better than what I'd been doing.

In phys ed, I was given a new badminton partner, Jake Elway, who rarely spoke to anybody and was a total klutz. I knew we had no chance of winning, so I guess I relaxed and played fairly well.

I'd seen Janice in the halls at school, but she wouldn't even look at me. Once I saw her with Scott.

At home, life followed a pattern. I went out a few times for cokes and to a movie with Ernie, and I watched a bit of TV, and Ernie and I worked with Todd on Monday night, and went to house group on Tuesday night; but other than that I worked on schoolwork, read my Bible, and didn't say much. House group was great. It was the first time I can remember where people actually seemed to want to hear about how I felt and what I was thinking. Well, maybe that's not quite true. Sandy and I used to talk about things like that. Only—well, I guess he used to be more practical than me. He used to think my ideas were dumb. Maybe that's why I stopped telling him what I was thinking.

Anyway, Andrew and the others really seemed to want to hear what I thought and to answer my questions about the Bible and so on. And I found myself sharing things I hadn't even really known myself. Several of them even asked to read my story and told me I should do more writing. And I also started to get interested in their lives—not just the surface stuff, but how they really felt and what was really happening in their lives. I found myself praying, especially for Doria, who was having the worst time with her father's arrest and all. It put my own problems into a different perspective.

At home, Dad barely spoke to me. He was really following his program of leaving me alone. Either that or he just didn't care any more. Sandy didn't say much either, although I caught him staring at me now and then as if trying to figure out what I was up to.

The weekend passed smoothly. I didn't say anything about going to church. Ernie brought a tape again and Mom and I listened to it together.

The next week I pulled off a 72 on a science quiz, another A on some questions on a story in English, and a C+ on a history essay. My running was settling into a pattern, and I felt good about it.

No one spoke to me much, other than Ernie. I saw Janice a couple of times in the halls. Once she said, "Hi, preacher," as she went past. The other times she ignored me. Ernie heard she'd been at Scott's on the weekend.

I was working so hard on my schoolwork that Todd finally told me to lighten up. He said if all I did was school work and Bible-reading, something would probably burst. So Ernie and I went to a movie one night and to an arcade after school twice.

But the fact was that I didn't feel overwhelmed by the work I was doing. In fact, I was almost enjoying myself. Mr. McNeely and Mr. Anderson both encouraged me. And Todd answered my questions from my Bible reading whenever we met to work on math.

And the cuts and bruises on my face healed, so I began to look like my normal self again.

But I really wasn't my normal self. It's funny. A month ago I would have thought that living as I now was would have been totally boring. But as I thought of going to parties at Scott's and hanging around in the arcade and just driving around and going to cafes, that seemed boring. I wouldn't go back to it for anything. I really was becoming a new person!

Then, just after I'd gone to bed on a Thursday night, the doorbell rang. The bell was followed immediately by someone banging on the door.

I turned my light on.

"It's likely one of your friends," Sandy said sarcastically. "You'd better get up."

"Dad's up," I said as I heard footsteps going down the stairs.

A second later, Dad yelled my name. I pulled on a pair of jeans and went downstairs.

Three cops were standing in the front hall.

"Shane Donahue?" the closest one asked.

"Yeah," I said, wondering if they'd found Ted.

"Shane Donahue, you are under arrest for robbery and assault. Anything you say may be used against you...." I listened as he went on about my right to call a lawyer and all that stuff. But my mind wasn't really hearing it. All I could focus on was that first line. I was under arrest for robbery and assault. Oh, God, now what?

One of the cops stayed with Mom and Dad while the other two went upstairs with me so I could put on a shirt and socks. They seemed wary, like they thought I was going to try to make a run for it or something. When they opened the door and found Sandy, they asked what he was doing there."

"I live here," Sandy said. "I'm his brother."

The way he said the word, you knew he'd rather be anything else.

One of the policemen watched us both like a hawk while the other checked the closet and the window.

They wouldn't even let me open the drawer to get my socks out. One of them had to do it.

Sandy stood there watching me, his mouth hard.

I looked over at him, but he wouldn't meet my eyes.

The cop handed me some socks and I sat on the bed to put them on. Then he went to the closet and grabbed a shirt. It was Sandy's, but neither of us said anything. I put it on and slowly did up the buttons.

"Hurry up," the cop said. "Let's go."

He motioned for me to go ahead of him and I did. But at the doorway, I turned. "Sandy?" I pleaded.

But he turned his back on me.

"I don't know what this is about," I said. "I didn't do anything. Sandy!"

The cop grabbed my arm and pulled me through the door and down the stairs. The other cop followed. When we got to the bottom, the first one handed me my shoes and I put them on.

Mom was holding my old jacket. Her eyes were full of tears.

Dad was back near the door to the kitchen. I looked at him, and, like Sandy, he turned his back on me.

"Dad?"

"I have only one son," he said, and he walked into the kitchen.

Mom started crying then, the sobs wrenching out of her.

The cop took my coat from her and handed it to me.

I put it on and shoved my feet into my shoes.

Then the cop who had been downstairs the whole time pulled my hands behind my back and put handcuffs on my wrists.

He took my arm, but I shook off his hand. I stepped toward Mom. "Mom, call Ernie. I swear I don't know anything about this. Tell Ernie to get Todd. Please."

The cop took my arm, and his grip was painful as he pushed me out the door. One of the other cops grabbed my other arm and the two of them hurried me toward three patrol cars that were parked at the curb. All three had flashing lights. One other cop was sitting in the lead car. Two more cops came from the back of the house.

I was propelled me into the back seat of the middle car. One of the cops got in with me.

I could still hear Mom crying.

16

We didn't talk in the cruiser. But when we got to head-quarters, they took me to a room where another cop joined us.

"All right, Shane. Why'd you do it?" the new cop asked.

I stared at him.

"There's no use pretending. We have proof that you were involved. All we want to know is who was in it with you?"

"Come on, kid, make it easier on yourself. Who was with you?"

"I don't know what you're talking about."

"Like fun you don't. Come on, kid, stop wasting our time. We've got you cold."

The cop who'd found my clothes for me said, "He's a tough guy, Sid. He won't squeal on his buddy. He wants to do time by himself."

"I didn't do anything."

"That's what the guilty ones all say." Sid leaned back in his chair as if satisfied.

"We'll get the truth out of you sooner or later," said the third cop, the one who'd driven the cruiser.

"Check your records," I said. "I'm clean."

"We already checked. You were beaten up a couple of weeks ago. You were questioned concerning the disappearance of Ted Cummings a couple of weeks ago, too. He hasn't shown up yet. Want to tell us some more about that?"

"There's nothing I can tell you."

"You said he'd run away. How do we know you aren't lying about that? Maybe you had something to do with his disappearance. Huh, kid?"

I was getting more scared by the minute.

But I was also thinking clearer. "I'm not saying anything till I have a lawyer."

"You heard the kid, Billy," Sid said. "He wants a lawyer. So who's your lawyer, kid?"

"My name is Shane," I said, "not 'kid.' And I've never needed a lawyer. But I have a friend who might know one. Can I call him?"

"Isn't your old man getting you a lawyer?" The cop called Billy, who'd been the one who arrested me, was being sarcastic. He'd heard what my dad said about having only one son.

I hung my head.

"So who's your lawyer, kid?" Sid repeated.

I didn't say anything.

"What's that you said? My hearing isn't so good."

"I don't have one."

"Well, let's talk about it in the morning, then. I think a few hours alone might loosen your tongue."

Sid jerked his head toward the third cop and he led me, still handcuffed, to what he called a holding cell. He took off the handcuffs and told me to get a good night's sleep.

It was a long time before I got to sleep. And I don't think you could have called it good.

In the morning, somebody brought me some toast and a cup of coffee.

Then a different cop came and asked me if I was ready to tell them about the robbery. I said I had to call my lawyer.

He took me to a phone in the corridor.

"I don't know his number," I said. "It's at home."

"You get two calls. Do what you want." He sounded bored.

I called Ernie's house, but there was no answer. I didn't know what to do next. Todd would be at work, and I didn't remember the name of his office.

Then I remembered Andrew had given me a card with his number on it. I had no idea what I'd done with the card he'd given me. Except—the pants I'd grabbed were the ones I'd worn to church the one time I'd gone. And that was when he'd given me the card. Was it possible?

With some difficulty because of the handcuffs, I reached into my pockets, one after the other, praying hard that the card was still there. It was likely Mom had washed them.

I felt something in the back pocket and pulled it out. It had been through the wash all right, but I could still make out the phone number.

I dialed the number, not really expecting an answer. I knew he was a college student, so there was a chance he wasn't at classes, but....

A woman answered. She spoke Chinese, I guess, and not much English. I said I was looking for Andrew and a moment later a man's voice answered. He spoke English better than her, but not as well as Andrew.

The cop said something about my taking too long.

Okay God, now what?

"Andrew is not here just now," the man said. "I am his father. Shall I take a message for him?"

"Yes, please. I don't want to bother him, and maybe there's nothing he can do, but I'm in jail and I don't—" I felt like something was stuck in my throat. Tears stung my eyelids. Not now, stupid. You can't break down now.

"Did I hear you say you are in jail?" the man asked.

I took a deep breath. "Yes. Look, can you just tell Andrew that Shane Donahue called and I'm in jail. I don't know why. They think I did something, but I didn't. I thought—I don't know what I thought—I don't know who else to call—"

"Are you the Shane who has recently been attending Andrew's house group?"

"Yes. I've—"

"I see." There was a moment of silence. Then he continued, "I think perhaps I may be of more use to you than Andrew in this instance. Which station are you in?"

Half an hour later, I was sitting in a small room opposite Andrew's father, a short, wrinkled man, who just happened to be an attorney.

"Mr. Hwang, I'm not even sure what I'm being charged with. They said something about robbery and assault."

"As far as I have been able to ascertain, a convenience store was robbed last night and the clerk was badly hurt. The police apparently have some evidence that links you with the crime."

"But I didn't do it! I was at home studying all night."

"Were you alone?"

I had to think back. Mom had worked from one until nine, so she got home at nine-thirty. Dad had gone out for a while to get some new tires for the car. He'd been gone from seven until after Mom was home. And Sandy had gone over to Kathy's house right after supper. "I was alone from about seven to nine-thirty."

"The store was robbed at eight-forty-five."

I swore. Then I saw the look on Mr. Hwang's face.

"I'm sorry. It just came out." I stood and paced around the small room. "So I have no alibi. But I still didn't do it. Why are they so sure I did?"

"They did not see fit to tell me, other than to say they had hard evidence."

"What does that mean?"

"A positive ID from a witness, fingerprints, a weapon or something else that clearly belongs to you that was found at the scene of the crime...."

"They can't identify me because I wasn't there. And there are no fingerprints for the same reason."

"So it must be something belonging to you."

"Something that belongs to me." I thought about it. "That would mean somebody was framing me."

"It might."

I turned and went up to face him. "Mr. Hwang, I didn't do it. I was home studying. I know my reputation isn't very good, but I've changed in the past month. I really have."

He leaned back and looked up at me. "Shane, my son has talked much about you, and we have prayed for you together, he and I. You have no reason to worry. I believe you."

Tears threatened. But he had to know the worst. "My father thinks I'm guilty. So does my brother."

"And your mother?"

"I don't know. Last Sunday she said I'd given her the courage to ask Jesus into her life. And now this. I don't know what she's thinking."

A cop knocked at the door and Mr. Hwang got up and went over to talk with him. Then he came back to me.

"Shane, go with the officer. Do not be difficult. I will see if you have been formally charged yet, and if so I will do what I can about arranging bail. That is if your friends who are now here have not done so already. The officer said that two young men—Todd and Ernie—are here."

I shut my eyes for a moment. Mom must have called Ernie, then, and he and Todd had come. Even if there wasn't anything they could do, at least I didn't have to face this completely alone.

Mr. Hwang went out and the cop took me back to the holding cell and left me there.

Despite Mr. Hwang's coming, and Todd and Ernie's, too, I sat there feeling sick. Not throwing-up kind of sick—the scared kind. The police and my family believed I had done something really awful, and there was nothing I could do about it. I know you're just supposed to tell the truth and if you're innocent everything will be okay. But, well, I also know that sometimes innocent people are found guilty.

I had to rely on Mr. Hwang. But would he be able to help me? And how could I pay him? Would my dad help out if I was found innocent?

I felt like crying, but what good would that do?

Getting mad wouldn't do anything, either.

My mind went back to that rally and the speakers I'd listened to then. I remembered that life hadn't been all roses for them. Especially the lady. I remembered how I'd felt when I realized God loved me. Had he stopped loving me? Or did he have some reason for letting me go through this?

I began to pray, asking him what I should do and begging him to help me. And asking him to show me how to act. I'd started reading Acts recently and I remembered that Peter and John had been thrown in prison for preaching about Jesus, and they had refused to stop. And Stephen had been stoned to death for talking about Jesus.

All of I sudden, I felt better. Not jumping up and down better, but better. I realized that God could still be in control. Maybe there was a reason for me to be in jail.

And Mr. Hwang. Was it just an accident that the one person I had thought to call happened to have a lawyer for a father? No way.

I started thinking about the evidence the police had. Something of mine. And then I remembered. My jacket! I knew it hadn't just vanished into the snow.

When mom had sewn the tear in my sleeve, she'd also written my initials on the label inside the neck. Could whoever found the jacket have used it to get me in trouble?

The whole thing became crystal-clear. Keith and Scott and the others had been angry because I'd turned to God and away from them. So they had framed me. I was in trouble, just like Peter and John, not because I'd done something wrong, but because I'd done something right!

But how could I prove it? Would anyone believe me?

A little while later, a cop appeared and told me I was getting out for now. I followed him to an outer room. Mr. Hwang was there, with Ernie and Todd.

When he saw them, the cop gave me a funny look. I guess he wondered why a white guy was getting out of jail to go with two black guys and an oriental.

I started to laugh. I don't know what got into me—maybe just the joy I felt at seeing them there—but I said to the cop, "It's okay. This is my family. We're all God's children."

He didn't say anything; just gave us all a searching look before leaving the room.

My friends were all smiling. Mr. Hwang explained that I would be having a hearing on Monday, and that I had been released into his custody until then. He also confirmed my suspicions that part of the evidence they had was my jacket.

"But I lost it the night I got beat up! I haven't seen it for over two weeks!"

"Do you have any witnesses?"

"Well, my mom knows I lost it, but I don't know if they'd believe her. Janice knows. She couldn't find it, so I didn't have anything to wear from the hospital! But since she's mad at me, I guess she might lie about it."

"Shane, there's something else. Something even more incriminating."

"What?"

"A positive ID on your car."

"My car, But—"

He held up his hand. "That's not all. The robber wore a black ski mask and took the money from the cash register in a paper bag. They found a ski mask and a paper bag of money stuffed under the back seat of your car. The police figure about half the money is there."

I've never been kicked by a horse, but I think I know how it feels.

Todd came and put his arm around me. I sagged against him.

"We'll get them, Shane," Ernie said. "Somebody's framed you."

"Keith and Scott," I mumbled. "It has to be them."

"We'll find some way to prove it."

We were walking out of the police station, Todd's arm still around me, when I saw the cop who'd come to talk to me about Ted. The female cop who'd said she was a Christian.

I broke away from Todd and ran over to her.

"I'm Shane Donahue," I said.

"I remember you. How's it going?"

"Not so hot. Have you found out anything about Ted?"

"No sign of him."

"Could anything have happened to him?"

"You mean like he'd been hurt or something?"

"Yes."

"Hospitals would let us know."

"Oh. So as far as you know, he's okay?"

"As far as we know. Why?"

"I just wondered. I was arrested last night."

"What for?"

"Robbery and assault. I didn't do it."

"You know they all say that."

"How could I show I was framed? I mean, how could I show it so the police would believe me?"

"Who framed you?"

"Remember how I was beat up when you came to my house? You noticed I hadn't fought back?"

"I remember."

"I think the same guys set me up now."

"You got any proof?"

"No, they've done too good a job. They used my car, and they left some stuff in it. And they left my jacket behind so it would be found."

"You expect the police to believe somebody hates you enough to go to all that trouble to frame you?"

"You saw what they did to me before."

She looked past me, her eyes staring at nothing. Then she looked straight at me. "All right, suppose they framed you. There's nothing to prove it, right? Just your word against a lot of hard evidence?"

"That's right."

"Then I'll be honest. There are only two things that could help you. A witness who heard them planning or saw them doing the robbery and can identify them. Or a confession by one of the ones who framed you. And by the way, there have to be witnesses to a confession. Your word alone wouldn't be worth anything."

"Yeah, I've learned that already."

"There's really very little you could do. Get a good lawyer. Maybe hire a private detective. It's not a job for amateurs."

Forcing out a "Thanks," I turned away so she wouldn't see the disappointment I felt.

She started off, then turned and fumbled in her purse. "Here's my number. Call me if you think of anything, or if you have a question. Ask for Officer Martel. And Shane, whatever you do, be careful. If you're talking about the convenience store that was robbed last night, you're talking nasty."

"I didn't do it."

She looked me in the eyes again. "I sure hope not."

Mr. Hwang had gone, leaving me to ride with Todd and Ernie. I realized Ernie should be at school and Todd had a job.

"You guys shouldn't have come down. You've got other places you should be."

"No place more important," Todd said. "But I think I'll drop both of you off and get to my office. I'll call tonight and maybe we can get together to figure this out. You really think your friends framed you?"

"Had to be them."

"What about Sandy?" Ernie said.

"What did you say?"

"I said, could it have been Sandy?"

"No way."

"Just wondering. I heard something about him at school yesterday."

"What did he do now? Win another trophy?"

"No. It was about who he's dating tonight."

"Yeah? Who?"

"Janice."

"Janice? You mean—Janice? Janice Hopkins?"

"You got it."

"I don't believe it!"

"Doesn't matter what you believe." Ernie shrugged. "It's true."

"So it was him she wanted all along! And he's likely dating her just to show me he can have whatever he wants! Well, they deserve each other!"

Todd dropped us both off at Ernie's house so Ernie could get his books. Then we took Ernie's car to my house. Sure enough, my car was gone. So was Dad's.

But Mom was in the house. I had to knock because for some reason I had failed to take my keys to the police station with me. Mom opened the door and peered out like she was scared it would be more bad news. When she saw me, she gave a little scream and then she flung the door open and grabbed me. It had been a long time since she hugged me like that. I guess that was my fault. I wouldn't have let her. But this time I didn't mind. In fact, I hugged her back.

She was crying again. After a few minutes, we went inside and I got her to sit down.

Ernie made her some tea while I told her what had happened. I said I'd been framed, and she seemed to accept that.

"Your dad," she said. "He's so—angry. He doesn't know what to do. He says he won't lift a finger to help you."

She started crying again, but I told her God would take care of me and she stopped crying and sat there staring at me as if she didn't recognize me.

Ernie brought in the tea, and then he made us all sand-wiches for lunch. We took our time. Mom calmed down, and we talked a little about how we could prove I'd been framed. The only problem was none of us had any ideas and Mom was scared stiff I'd get hurt, so she didn't want me to do anything.

We promised that we wouldn't do anything without telling her first.

Mom had called the library and said she was sick, but we convinced her she'd be better working than worrying, and she went to get dressed. We dropped her at the library and then went to school.

I guess Sandy hadn't wanted to spread around the fact that his brother had been arrested, so no one said anything. After class, I went to see Mr. Anderson. I'd missed running that morn-ing. He was in his office off the gym. I tapped on the door and was told to come in.

"I'm sorry about this morning. I—I had something come up. I couldn't be here."

"Okay."

"I—I hope you aren't angry. I didn't want to miss."

He smiled. "I said it was okay. I meant it was okay."

"Good."

"I'll see you Monday morning?"

"I'll do my best to be here."

"Fine."

"That is...are you sure you want to? I mean, I wouldn't want you wasting your time on me."

"Can I let you in on a little secret, Shane?"

"Huh?"

"When we have our first track meet, you're going to demonstrate to a lot of those guys what it feels like to eat dust. And that reminds me. How are those grades doing?"

"Pretty good."

"You passing everything yet?"

"Working on it."

"Well, keep it up. And if you need any help, tell me. I know a few things other than phys ed."

I thanked him, then went to find Ernie. We decided to go for hamburgers so we could talk some more.

"If I'm not in jail, I've got to get a job," I said in disgust. "I can't sponge off you for the rest of my life."

"Nope," Ernie said as he stuffed a huge bite into his mouth.

"I know I can't."

"Not for the rest of your life. A few more weeks or months is okay."

"No, it isn't."

"Well, let's worry about that later. Right now we have to keep you out of jail."

"What Officer Martel said was that I needed a witness or a confession. I don't know how I could find a witness. For starters, neither of them would let anybody know what was happening. So I need a confession. How can I get one?"

"You can't go near those guys."

"I have to. Otherwise, I'm dead meat."

"What we need is a plan of some sort."

But though we racked our brains, we couldn't come up with anything.

Ernie drove me home. I didn't know what would happen there, and he told me I was welcome to come to his house if my dad threw me out.

When I walked into the kitchen, they all stared at me. But neither Dad nor Sandy spoke.

"I told your dad the police had let you go," said Mom.

"I have a hearing Monday," I replied.

"Thanks for telling us," Sandy sneered.

"Thanks for believing in me," I said softly.

Sandy's head jerked up, and after staring at me for a minute, he left the room.

Dad took another helping of potatoes and ignored me.

"Walt," Mom's voice quivered. "He's not guilty. He didn't do what they said he did."

He kept eating.

"Don't worry about it, Mom," I said. "I've got some home-work to do. That's if it's okay for me to stay here. Is it?"

He kept eating potatoes, acting like he was deaf.

"Did you hear him, Walt? Your son wants to know if it's okay for him to stay here in his home?"

17

"Dad, I'm sorry I'm not the son you wanted. I'd like to be like Sandy, but I can't. I know it's been my fault this past year, but I've changed ever since I found God, and I—"

"I told you to forget all that God stuff!" he bellowed.

"You said I couldn't go to church on Sunday, and I haven't. But I'm not going to turn my back on God." I spoke evenly, trying to keep control.

Dad's face was red with anger. "All right, you smart aleck. Let me tell you a thing or two. My parents were so-called Christians. And they went by the "Good Book" in everything they did. They had no money because they gave it all away. They had no fun because they weren't allowed to do anything. Their list of "shall nots" was longer than your arm. And I was never allowed to do anything, either. Once, when I was about ten, some kids beat me up because I was dressed funny—hand-me-downs because all our money went to the church—and I tried to stand up for myself! I got a cracked bone in my hand from hitting one of them. You know what my parents were concerned about? Not that they'd tried to beat me up! Not that I was hurt! But that I'd defended myself! They said I should have turned my other cheek! Can you believe that?"

"But, Dad—"

"Be quiet! I won't have that God stuff shoved down my throat, and for sure not by my own son! Maybe I don't have a good education, but I've got a decent job and you've got everything any kid needs. All it takes is for you to stand on your own two feet. If you aren't guilty, you just tell the truth. You don't need any God, believe me!"

"Walt, you're wrong." Mom said as she stepped between Dad and me.

"I'm wrong, am I? Since when do you tell me I'm wrong?"

"Since I asked God to come into my life and change me."

"So you're doing it, too? Why? What more do you need?"

"Oh, Walt, you can't blame God for what your parents did. Maybe they misunderstood. People make mistakes. But that doesn't mean God does."

"I can't believe you'd turn on me this way!"

"Walt, look at him! Look at your son! A month ago, he was headed for trouble. Walt, you know he was. And you didn't know what to do. Remember that night you slapped him? Remember how angry you were, and how helpless you felt?"

"I didn't!"

"Yes, you did. You'll never admit it, but you did. And you said to me we'd done everything we could for him, and he'd have to stand or fall on his own."

"Yeah. So what?"

"So he stood, Walt! Look at him now! He's passing his tests at school; he's not going around with those wild kids any more; he's home studying instead of out drinking until all hours of the night; he's doing things to help around the house without even being asked! He isn't the same person he was, Walt! You must see that!"

"Well, if he's doing so great—?"

"Ask him why, Walt! Ask him what made the difference! He'll tell you it was God! Walt, any God that can turn my child's life around this way has to be the kind of God we need to know more about. We need to go to church with him instead of keeping him away. We need to—"

"I don't believe God had a thing to do with it. If he has changed, it's because he decided it was time he straightened up and stood on his own two feet."

"That isn't true, Dad," I said quietly. "I was thinking about killing myself. Or else running away with Ted. But when some people said God could help me, I thought it wouldn't hurt to give him a try first. Dad, things have happened that couldn't be just accidents. He's in control, and I feel so much better."

"Yeah? So how come we had police here last night to arrest you? You feeling good about that? You think letting you get arrested is God's way of looking after you?"

"I don't care what it looks like," I insisted. "There's some reason for this. He knows what he's doing."

"You don't know what you're talking about! Maybe when you go to jail you'll come to your senses. But by then it'll be too late. Get me a beer, Elise! My show's on." He went into the living room and turned on the TV.

I shrugged and went upstairs. He hadn't thrown me out. That was something.

Sandy was in our room, but we didn't speak.

I remembered what Ernie had overheard about Sandy. He had a date tonight with Janice.

"Got a date tonight, huh?" I asked casually.

He didn't answer.

"Big one?"

"None of your business."

"Okay, but I wouldn't wear that shirt"

"Why not this shirt?" Sandy asked, half angry, half exasperated.

"It looks too stuffy for a big date. Fine for going to meet your future in-laws, though."

Sandy looked at the shirt in his mirror, then took it off.

"Wear the red one. That'll get her attention."

"I'll choose my own clothes if you don't mind."

"Just trying to be helpful."

"Can it."

I groaned as Sandy took out a pink shirt. "Not that one!"

"There's nothing wrong with it."

"It clashes with your eyes."

"Be quiet."

"How about the green one? It looks good."

Sandy pulled out the green shirt. "There! Are you happy?"

"I'm not sure. It might clash with her eyes."

"Her eyes are brown."

"Are they? I never noticed."

Sandy paused, his shirt half-buttoned. "Who told you?"

"Ernie heard two of your friends laughing about it."

"So?"

"So—nothing. Keith was welcome to Marietta and you're welcome to Janice."

"I don't think I would compare the two."

"Oh, I don't know. They've got a lot in common."

"What's that supposed to mean?

"Nothing."

"You said yourself it was me she wanted to date first."

"You said it, but I agree. No hard feelings."

"Are you going out?"

"No."

"I suppose you're going to stay home and do homework."

"Yeah, I suppose I am."

"You used to—"

"What?"

"Never mind." Sandy had finished buttoning his shirt. He shoved his wallet into his pocket and went out of the room.

I read my Bible for a while, then worked on my English. But after a while I grew restless. My mind kept coming back to Keith and Scott. One or both of them had framed me and I had to prove it. But how?

Ernie was at work tonight. We were going to get together with Todd in the morning and see if we could come up with some kind of plan.

I guess I fell asleep trying to think of a plan, because the next thing I knew Mom was bending over me calling my name.

"Shane, there's a call for you. A Mr. Hopkins. He wanted to know if you were here and when I said you were, he insisted on talking to you now. It's past midnight and your dad is very angry. The phone woke him up."

I stumbled downstairs, half-asleep, wondering what on earth this was all about.

"Shane?" said a deep male voice.

"Yeah."

"Where's my daughter, you no-good—!" He used a string of obscenities.

I waited until he was finished. "Who is this?"

"If she's over there I'll skin you alive! And if you've left her some place—!"

"Who did you say you were?"

"Who is it? Janice's father, that's who it is! Who'd you think it was, you louse! Now where's my daughter!"

"How would I know where—?" I suddenly remembered that she had been going out with Sandy. I guess Mr. Hopkins didn't realize there were two of us. "She went out with my brother, not me. We're twins."

"Of all the lying—"

"Just a second. Let me see if he's here." Wide awake now, I ran upstairs and looked at Sandy's bed. Still made. I ran back downstairs. "Mr. Hopkins, Sandy isn't in yet. I expect Janice will be home any minute now."

"She told me she'd be in by midnight. It's a quarter to one. And what's this about you having a twin? I don't believe any of it. You get my daughter home here or I'm calling the cops!" He slammed the receiver down.

Now what? I didn't think the police would take him seriously. After all, Janice was sixteen and it wasn't that late. But still....

"Shane?" Mom's voice came silently from the stairs. "Is anything wrong?"

"The girl Sandy's out with—her dad wants her home. Do you know where they were going?"

"Just to a movie. I think. I'm surprised he isn't in yet. He said he wouldn't be late. Oh, Shane, do you think something has happened?"

"It's not that late, Mom. They likely went to eat or went to somebody's house. Or they might have run out of gas. You never know." I'd used all sorts of excuses in the past, when I still made excuses.

"Should we do anything?"

"Well, it's pretty late to phone. I could maybe drive over to a couple of his friends' houses. If I see cars there, I could go in. If there's a party or something." Slight chance, but at least I could tell Mr. Hopkins I had tried.

Mom nodded. Because I'd fallen asleep while reading, I was still dressed, so I grabbed some shoes and a jacket and started out. Then I remembered. "Mom?"

"Yes, Shane?"

"I don't have a car. The cops took mine."

She went and found her purse. "Here," she said, holding out her keys. "Be careful."

"But I thought Sandy has the car?"

"No. Wilf was going away for the weekend, so he loaned Sandy his car."

"Dad wouldn't want me to take ours."

"He wouldn't want anything to happen to Sandy, either."

"Okay, Mom.

As I started outside, she called softly, "I'll be praying."

Half an hour later, I was ready to quit. There were no lights on at Paul's or anyone else I could think of who might have had a party Sandy would go to. And the two restaurants where Sandy was likely to go were both closed. I stopped at a pay phone and called the Hopkins' house.

Janice answered.

"It's Shane. I just wanted to make sure you were home. Your dad called looking for you."

"I'm home," she replied. "And when you see your brother, which I expect won't be for a while, you can tell him that I don't see any difference between you. You're both creeps!" She hung up.

"Now what?" I wondered. But at least I knew Sandy was okay. At least, I assumed he was.

There was nothing else I could do, so I went home. Mom was still up, but she seemed satisfied when I said everything was okay. I undressed and got ready for bed, and was just about to turn out the light when I heard Sandy at the front door. I had locked the door when I came in, expecting Sandy would have his key. But he seemed to be fumbling around. Then there was a very soft rap. I went down.

"Forget your key?" I asked as I opened the door.

"Shut up."

I was about to say something about guys who stay out with girls and get the girl's father mad when I realized he was in a bad mood. I guess Janice will do that to you.

"What happened?" I asked, trying to make my voice sound uninterested.

"None of your business, you—you—jerk!"

"What did I do now?"

"That's the last time I try to help you out!"

"Help me?" My voice rose. "Your going out with Janice is supposed to help me?"

He didn't say anything. Just hauled off and hit me square on the jaw. I went down onto the hall carpet and sat there wondering if he'd lost his mind. "What was that for?" I yelled.

Dad and Mom appeared at the top of the stairs: Mom asking what was wrong, Dad shouting at us to go to bed. Did we know what time it was? Was there a conspiracy to keep him from getting any sleep tonight?

"I'm sleeping in the basement," Sandy said. "I should have done that a long time ago."

"Go ahead. See if I care."

He went upstairs slowly, walking like his feet hurt—like maybe he'd had to walk a fair ways. And no keys. Had Janice...? Naw, she couldn't have. But I got up and went to the dining room window to look out at the spot on the driveway where Sandy would have parked Wilf's car. It was empty. My jaw ached where he'd hit me, but I had to laugh, smothering the sound with a place mat so Sandy wouldn't hear and get madder. She had done it to him, too—made him walk home. From where, I wondered. And why?

I heard Sandy come back to the main floor and then go down the basement steps. Nothing more I could do tonight. He was as sore as a bear with a thorn in its paw. May as well go to bed and get some sleep. I still had my own problems to think about in the morning.

Ernie called around ten. Mom came to wake me up, and I asked her to tell him I'd be right over.

As I was getting out of bed, Sandy walked in. He was wearing the clothes he'd worn last night and he still looked angry.

"Where are you going?" he asked as I started dressing.

"Ernie's."

"You aren't going anywhere until we've had a talk."

I pulled on a T-shirt.

"Did you hear me?"

"I heard you."

"Well?"

"Well, what? What do you want to talk about?"

"I'm sick and tired of this. You're not leaving until we've settled it."

"Settled what? What are you talking about?"

"I took Janice out last night because I wanted to know the truth about what's been going on. Now I want to talk to you!"

"Just what did you think Janice could tell you?"

"She told me quite a few things. Like what good parties your friend Scott gives. And how she thinks Keith is so cool. And how since you got religion you've turned into some kind of prude who wouldn't let her have any fun. And how Keith and Scott and some of your other *friends*," he spat out the word, "beat you up."

Where did he get off sounding so righteous? "Yeah, that's right! And when I got beat up you said you wanted to thank whoever did it! So, are you going to?" I yelled.

"Sure, I wanted to thank them!"

"Well, you don't need my permission for that. So why don't you leave me alone!"

"You jerk! You totally stupid idiot jerk! I hate your guts!" He turned away.

"I know you do." I wasn't yelling any more.

He spun around. "Is that what you think? You think I hate you?"

"You do, don't you." It was a statement, not a question."

"Why shouldn't I? You hate me!"

"I never said I hated you!"

"You didn't have to say it! You chose to be with people like Keith and Ted and Marietta instead of me! And this past month, you spent all your time with Ernie! You didn't care how I felt. Did you forget we were twins, Shane? Every time I tried to help you, you pulled away from me. And then, when you started changing, when you seemed to be doing better, you didn't even want to tell me what had happened! You're my twin, Shane!" His eyes were filling with tears, but whether of rage or something else I didn't know.

"I thought you'd laugh at me," I said stupidly. "You did, that day Paul and Wilf were here."

"You shut me out! After that I didn't care what they did. Or what I did. Maybe I even wanted to hurt you, the way you were hurting me. How do you think I felt last night taking Janice out just so I get a clue about what's going on in my own brother's life!"

"You could have asked me!"

"Yeah, right. And I'm sure you would have told me everything. Just like you told me all about how Keith and Scott and the others beat you up!"

"I would have told you if I thought you cared!"

"Well, I did care!"

We stood there glaring at each other.

"Shane...." He moved closer. "This is getting us nowhere. I don't hate you. I just don't know what to do."

"I don't hate you, either."

"You act like you do."

"You started it."

"You're crazy! You're the one that started hanging around with Keith and those guys. I haven't changed. It was you!"

I shook my head. Then, quietly, I said, "You didn't need me any more."

"What are you talking about. Of course, I—" He stopped and thought for a moment, his eyes never leaving mine. "Shane, did you really think that?"

I nodded.

"Shane...I didn't...."

"You had so many friends."

"But they were your friends, too."

"No, they weren't. I was just one of your many admirers. You didn't need me."

"I never wanted anyone to be more important than you, Shane. Believe me. I like my friends, but they're only friends. You're my twin! Shane, I've been miserable these past months."

"I have, too, Sandy." I looked at him, wondering how much he would understand. " But...well, I think there were some things I needed to learn for myself. No matter how much we look alike, we aren't the same. We don't think the same. We don't want the same things. Heck, none of your friends even like me."

"So they'll learn to like you or—or they don't need to be my friends."

"No, it's more than that, Sandy. I've been thinking about it a lot. I needed to find out who I am."

"Shane, I just want my brother back. The one I used to know."

"I don't think it can be like it was before. I spent a lot of years following in your shadow, doing whatever you did. And that's wrong for me. But I would like to be friends again, Sandy."

"There's a lot about you I don't understand. All this stuff about God. I don't think I know you at all."

I looked at the floor. I wasn't totally sure I knew myself just then.

"Shane, what about the police? What are you going to do? Janice says you had the jacket when you came home."

"She's lying."

"Shane, if you did it, you'd be better to confess. It would go easier on you."

"You think I did it? Robbed a corner store and hit an old man?"

"I know you needed money and—and I know you've stolen before. From me, and Mom. And you've done other things.... "

"I didn't do this."

"I sure hope not. I just don't know any more. Janice says—"

"Ignore anything Janice says."

"I told her she was lying. To see what she'd say.'

"And?"

"She threw a couple of tapes out of the car window, and when I got out to get them she took off with the car. I assume it's at her place. She wasn't very happy with me. She realized I was only going out with her to find out about you." Anger surged within him again. "Do you know how stupid I felt dating a girl I don't even like just to find out what was going on in my own brother's life?"

"I'm sorry, Sandy. But do you know how it feels to have my brother think I robbed a store and beat up someone?"

"I don't want to think it. I don't want it to be true, either. But you've done so many dumb things this past year, I don't know what to believe any more."

I decided getting angry wasn't going to solve anything. "Sandy, do you really think if I had robbed the store I would have left my jacket there for the cops to find?"

"That's the thing that keeps bugging me. You may be dumb, but you aren't stupid."

I smiled. That was a true brotherly compliment.

"So what are you going to do?" he asked.

"Get together with Ernie and Todd and try to figure something out."

"I don't know them. I mean, I know who Ernie is, but that's about all.

"You can come with me if you'd like. I'm already late."

"I don't know."

"You still think I did it?"

"I still—I don't know what I think."

"Suit yourself." I turned to finish dressing.

"I guess I've spent most of my life getting you out of trouble," said Sandy. "I suppose one more time won't hurt. If you're sure you want me?"

"What are we waiting for?"

"A car," he said. "Neither of us has one."

While Sandy had a quick shower, I phoned Ernie. He drove us to Janice's. Wilf's car was parked out front, the keys in the ignition. Lucky it was still there.

Then Sandy followed Ernie and me to Ernie's house, where Todd was waiting.

On the way, I told Ernie that Sandy was coming to see if he could help.

Ernie was philosophical. "Todd said God can bring good out of bad. Maybe that's what he's doing here."

"Yeah. Like maybe it would be okay if I spent the rest of my life in prison just as long as Sandy isn't mad at me any more?"

18

When we got to Ernie's, we followed him into the living room. I was shocked to find not only Todd waiting for us, but Alicia, Andrew, Brad, Doria, Susan, Hans, and Angie—all the members of my house group. Andrew said they had come to help, and perhaps we should begin by praying since God was the one who would know what was best to do.

I glanced sideways at Sandy and grinned at his look of astonishment. I remembered how recently he had said something to me about my not having friends. Turned out he was wrong.

So we sat down. I don't know what Sandy thought, but all we did for the next hour was pray.

Then I told them about Keith and Scott, and why I thought they'd framed me.

Todd had some questions. "It seems like somebody went to a lot of trouble just to frame you—robbing a store and beating up a man and then leaving half the money in the car—just so you would be blamed." He shook his head. "Are you sure there's nobody with a better reason?"

"None that I can think of."

"There's no one else who could have taken your jacket?"

"I know I grabbed it when we left the house. And Janice said she found her coat on the ground after the fight, but not mine. So somebody who was there must have taken it."

"Won't Janice swear that you didn't have the jacket?"

Sandy answered. "No. She's angry with him. She says Shane had the jacket. She said she's glad he's in trouble."

"Could Janice have done this herself?"

"She couldn't have stolen my car. Not by herself. She wouldn't know anything about starting it. And she wouldn't have been able to get inside the garage."

"She had no way to get a key?"

I remembered that she'd had my keys overnight. But that wouldn't have given her time to get a key made. Besides, I couldn't see her robbing a store or beating up someone.

"What about Marietta?" Ernie asked. "She's driven your car a few times. Did she have a key?"

"No, I don't—" I remembered something. "She knew where the key to the garage was kept. Janice didn't. I don't think anyone else did. Except maybe Ted.

"Ted couldn't be hanging around here, could he?"

"Nobody's seen him," I said. "Besides, why would he want to get me into trouble?"

"Maybe because you didn't go with him."

"I can't see him doing that," I said.

"You can see Keith doing it?" Ernie asked.

I started thinking about that. My first instinct had been to blame Keith, but now I wasn't so sure. If Keith were going to get back at me for besting him in the fight, he'd already done it by beating me up with Scott and the others. Why would he go to the trouble of framing me? And did he have enough brains to think of this. I shook my head.

"Not Keith," I said. "I just can't see it. He might want to beat me up, but I can't see him doing anything like this. Too much risk for him. And not enough satisfaction. He likes fighting in the open, not sneaking around in the background."

"Scott?" Ernie asked.

"Maybe," I said thoughtfully. "But why would he go to all this trouble to set me up? I didn't do anything to him."

Sandy had been very quiet up until now. "If it were just your jacket," he said, "I'd think anybody could have done it and worn your jacket because they happened to find it. And left it there to lead the cops astray. But the car—and leaving the money in the car—"

"It's really very strange," said Hans, who had been very quiet till now. "Half of the money left there to convict you. I think it would need someone who hates you very much to do this."

I thought immediately of Sandy. Yesterday, I might have said Sandy hated me that much. But now I knew better. My dad? Not in my wildest dreams could I see him doing this.

The others from my house group had been very quiet since we finished praying. They didn't know the people involved except from what I'd told them. But now Susan sat up straighter.

"Shane," she said thoughtfully, "I think this is someone you have scorned, perhaps. Someone who wants to hurt you but cannot do it in a normal way. Someone, for instance, who could not fight you face to face. Someone who is very, very angry with what you have done. Someone who has no need for money, but only revenge."

Janice? She had been mad at me for not being what she wanted, but I couldn't see that she'd been all that hurt. And while she did have a pretty active temper, I didn't see her as helpless. Not the way she's driven off on both Sandy and I and ripped up my Bible and all.

A memory of Marietta's face popped into my mind. I remembered the look in her eyes when I said she wasn't worth fighting for and that she had no class. And how she had made those deep scratches in my neck. I still had marks there. Marietta didn't need the money. Her dad owned a couple of bars and they had all they needed.

Marietta had been there the night Janice and I went to Scott's. She had been with Keith, but as I thought about it now, I realized she hadn't looked very happy. And her eyes had almost seemed to blaze anger out at me. She would have followed the guys out of the house that night. She would have recognized my jacket, maybe even put it on to keep warm. She would have kept it, hoping she could use it somehow. She couldn't fight me, not face to face. But I could easily imagine her trying to get even with me.

There was only one problem. Marietta hadn't robbed the store.

Who could she have convinced to do it for her? Somebody who did need money. Not Scott or Keith. Ted. It had to be Ted. But how could I prove it?

I quickly told the others what I was thinking. And then we prayed some more, asking God to show us what to do.

"The store clerk will be able to tell the cops that the guy was shorter than you," Ernie said. "Ted's a lot shorter than you are, and skinnier."

"He might be able to," Andrew said. "But don't forget, the robber was wearing a ski mask. And the clerk was likely very frightened. Witnesses aren't always reliable, especially when they are frightened. If the police tell the clerk they've arrested you and describe you to him, he may revise his first impressions. And I know my father says it's never good policy to badger a man who has been injured, even over something like the description of his assailant. It doesn't sit well with a jury."

"That's also assuming he recovers," Todd said. "What if he doesn't?"

"There must be some way," Brad said. "We need her to confess before witnesses."

"I could confront her," I suggested. "Tell her I know she did it. Scare her."

"It's better if you don't have to threaten her," Paul said.

We all sat there thinking. What could we possibly do to get the truth out?

"Scott's parents are away for the weekend," Ernie volunteered. "So there's a party tonight at his house."

"Marietta will be there," I said.

"Lots of witnesses," Sandy said.

"But what could we do to make her talk?"

"If I go there, I'll end up having to fight somebody," I said. "But Christians aren't supposed to fight. So what could I do?"

"I wouldn't say you're never supposed to fight," Todd said. "It's okay to defend yourself."

"But," Hans said, "it is always good to choose the best weapons."

"The armor of God," I said, remembering what Officer Martel had told me.

"Exactly!" Andrew said. "That's what we'll do!"

We all turned to stare at him.

"We will use the weapons we have. The sword of the Spirit, the helmet of salvation, the breastplate of faith, the shoes of the gospel of peace—all of them."

We continued to stare at him, none of us having a clue what he meant.

"We've been looking at this the way ordinary people would. But how does God operate? David defeated Goliath with a slingshot. Why? Because it wasn't David fighting Goliath at all. It was God. So let's let God do the battle. We will all go there tonight. And we will stand outside the house and we will pray. And Shane will go in, or perhaps they will come out, and he will tell them what has happened, and perhaps share what God has done in his life, and we will let God work."

We all stared at Andrew and then at each other. It was such a crazy idea. But it was the only idea we had.

Sandy didn't say anything. What do you say to a bunch of nut-cases? He went home a little while later, saying he had work to do but he'd go along tonight.

A few kids had to leave, but they planned to meet us that night at ten outside the house. Todd, Alicia, Ernie, Andrew, Susan, Brad, and I basically prayed all afternoon. When we weren't praying, we were working on what I would say.

I've no idea what Ernie's mom thought, especially when she offered to order pizza and Todd said he thought we should fast instead. I had no idea what that meant, but he told me that there are a number of places in the Bible where people were told to pray and fast—not eating—for especially important prayer requests.

Then Todd read the story of Joshua and the people of Israel taking the city of Jericho by marching around it and blowing trumpets. In other words, it wasn't anything they did. God did it all.

Only that wasn't true, either. I mean, they did blow those trumpets and march around the city every day for a week. They must have felt pretty dumb doing that.

I wondered if they felt as dumb as I would feel tonight.

At nine-thirty, just before we left, everybody gathered around me and each person put a hand on my head or back, and they all prayed for me, that I would have wisdom to know what to say, and that I would do what God wanted. It's hard to explain how I felt when they did that. Probably better than I'd ever felt in my life before. I remembered how alone I had felt only a few weeks before. And now I had friends who would give their whole Saturday just to help me out. But it wasn't only that. I really felt God was there, too. It's not a feeling I can explain. I think you have to experience it to understand.

I went with Ernie to pick up Sandy. He looked—I don't know—uncomfortable I guess. For maybe the first time ever.

"You really going to do this?" Sandy asked after he got in the back seat. "Go to Scott's house and stand outside praying?"

"Yes," I said.

"It sounds pretty dumb to me."

"Yeah, me, too," Ernie said. "Only..."

"Yeah?" I urged. "Only what?"

"Only wouldn't it be neat if it really works?"

"God is real," I said. "So if we follow what he says in the Bible, why shouldn't it work?"

"If you want to believe that," Sandy said, "go ahead. But don't expect me to believe it."

"You're here," I said.

"Because I said I'd come. But this is hardly what I expected to happen. However, when you come to your senses and decide you have to try something else, I'll be there."

"Thanks, Sandy. I appreciate that."

We had reached the street. There were a lot of cars, but Ernie found a spot, and within five minutes the others had all arrived and we were standing wondering what to do next.

"I think we surround the house," Andrew said. "In groups of two. And we pray. Out loud."

"Well, what are we waiting for?" Todd started forward.

"I'm not praying," Sandy said.

I said, "Come with Ernie and me."

So he followed us to the back of the house.

It felt really weird. But all around the house we started praying—that God would reveal the truth about what had happened—that Marietta and Ted and the other kids inside would come to know God—that no one would get hurt—and that God would be in control of everything.

How long we'd have stayed there, or what we'd have done when we were finished praying, I don't know. But we didn't have to worry about that. Someone must have looked out a window or something because after about twenty minutes the back door opened and Scott came out.

The light at the back door helped us see him, but we were in the shadows so he couldn't see us very well at all.

"What's going on out here?" he asked. "Who are you and what are you doing?"

I stepped forward so he could see me. "Scott, it's me. Shane."

He swore. "What are you doing out here?"

"Is Marietta here?" I asked, keeping my voice low and trying not to sound angry. Truth was I didn't feel angry. I felt sorry for her.

"Yeah, she's here. But she doesn't want to see you. Who are those other people?"

Ernie and Sandy stepped closer so he could see them. Andrew and Brad were on our left, Todd and Alicia on the right. The others were toward the front of the house.

"What are you doing out there?" Scott asked.

"Oh, we're, uh, just praying," I said.

Sandy snorted.

"Most of us are praying, " I said more accurately.

"You're what?"

"What's going on?" Keith asked as he muscled out beside Scott. "Who are you talking to? Shane? That you?"

I went up to within ten feet of the back door. At the same time, somebody opened the patio doors and kids started to crowd out.

"What's up, Shane?" Keith called out. "You want to fight or something?"

"No," I said. "I don't want to fight."

Somebody started clucking like a chicken.

"So why are you here?" Keith sounded puzzled.

Scott answered. "He says he's praying for us."

"Oh, that sounds good."

Janice came out of the crowd from the patio doors. She was wearing a red halter top and a very short, very tight black skirt with black stockings. She had on really high heels, the kind Marietta wears, and she was staggering.

"Hi, Shane. Did you come for me? Sorry. I've moved on to better things. Right Scotty?"

"Come here, baby."

She teetered over to Scott and he kissed her, then slapped her on the behind. "Get inside. You'll freeze out here."

She giggled like he'd said something hilarious, but she went in.

Keith was getting impatient. "It's cold out here, Shane. If you want to fight, fine. Otherwise I'm going in."

"You can go in," I said. "We're staying here."

"To pray?"

"Yes."

"Have fun!" he said, going inside and slamming the door.

"You can't stay here," said Scott. "It's our property. I can have you arrested for trespassing."

"Then we'll go out on the street out front. You don't own that."

"You're crazy. Nuts! What are you doing this for?"

"Did Marietta tell you Ted was around?"

"Ted? No. Nobody's seen Ted."

"Marietta saw him. Ask her."

"So what?"

"Ask her why she talked Ted into robbing a store, Scott. Ask her why she was willing to get Ted in trouble with the cops."

Scott swore at me and went inside. I could hear people praying, Ernie beside me. Oh, God, I prayed. Please let this work. I don't know what else to do.

The door opened and Keith came out again. "Shane, if you want to talk, come in. It's freezing out here."

We had come prepared for this. I had a small tape recorder in my pocket and a microphone connected to it taped to my chest. I just had to make sure my jacket was open.

"Okay," I said.

"I'm going with you," Sandy said.

I started to say I might be better to go alone, but I saw his face and thought better of it. He was out of his depth here, at least as far as the prayer part was concerned. But as backup in case this turned ugly, there was nobody I'd rather have with me.

We followed Keith inside.

In the kitchen, Scott was sitting on a kitchen chair with Janice on his knee. He was holding a glass to her lips and she was drinking and giggling. In between sips, she was kissing him.

Anger washed over me, but I held it down. This was one time I definitely could not afford to lose my cool.

So far, I hadn't seen Marietta. But that problem was solved immediately. She had been standing behind the door as we went in. "What are you doing here?" Her voice exploded shrilly in my ear.

I turned. "Looking for some answers."

"Well, nobody here wants you."

"No?"

Marietta tapped her heel angrily. "Don't be stupid. Keith, he's drunk."

"Marietta, I know what you did. You found my jacket and you decide to use it to get me in trouble. I don't know when or how you saw Ted, but you must have. Unless there's somebody else who would have needed the money enough to help you. But it was all your idea. Stealing my car and robbing the store, and making it look like I'd done it. Whose idea was it to beat up the clerk?"

"Get out of here!" she yelled. "Keith, get him out of here!"

"Sure." He came at me, fire in his eyes, thinking this was party time.

"I'm not going to fight you, Keith," I said.

He replied with a right to my stomach and a left to my chin and I went back against the door, gasping for breath.

"Come on, Shane. You turned into a wimp?"

Between breaths, I repeated what I'd just said. "I said I wasn't going to fight you. I want to talk to you."

He snapped my head back with a solid right and my head bounced against the door.

"You're an idiot!" Sandy yelled. "Come on, Keith. If he doesn't want to fight you, I will."

I yelled, "Sandy! No!"

He was in the middle of a swing when I jumped forward, and instead of hitting Keith his fist caught me hard on my arm and sent me flying into Keith.

Keith pushed me back against Sandy and I sort of stood there between them with both of them glaring at me.

"What is this, anyway?" Keith yelled in disgust. "What are you doing?"

"I'm trying to talk to you!" I yelled back. "I want to tell you something!"

"Well, why didn't you say so?"

"Can I sit down?"

"Yeah. You want a beer?"

"No. I just need a chair."

I sat down. Arms crossed, Sandy leaned against the door.

"Get out of here!" Marietta's voice was shrill.

"I just want to tell you a story," I said. "Then I'll leave."

"Well, I don't want to hear your story," she spat out at me.

"I do," Janice said. "I like stories."

Scott laughed. "Okay, Shane, make it quick. I've got better things to do tonight than listen to you and your sappy brother."

"Once upon a time there was a guy who liked a girl. And she liked him, too. But the problem was both of them were pretty mixed up. He didn't always act the way he should have. He was pretty selfish, in fact, thinking about himself instead of what was best for her.

"One day, she decided that she was tired of him and of his attitude, so she told him she wanted to break up, and that she was going to go out with one of his best friends. He was angry, not just because of her but because he was pretty mixed up about a lot of things. But he fought his friend, and when he won, he said he didn't care about the girl any more and his friend could have her."

"Nice story," said Marietta. "Now get out."

"This made the girl angry, and she wanted to get revenge. But she didn't know how.

"Then one day she found an opportunity. She got hold of the boy's jacket.

"Later, she talked to another friend of his who had bragged that he could survive on his own. Only he wasn't doing that well, and he needed money. The girl helped him steal his friend's car. I expect she convinced him his friend wouldn't mind. Then she drove the car and he robbed a store.

"Only the clerk got in the way and ended up getting hurt. The girl was scared, but not so scared she forgot what she wanted to do.

"She made sure the jacket was left for the police to find, and she left her half of the money and the ski mask in the car when they returned it.

"And then she very helpfully phoned in anonymously to let the police know the license number of the car."

"What on earth are you talking about?" Keith sounded annoyed more than anything.

Janice was still giggling, still drinking and kissing Scott. But she stopped to look at me. "That wasn't a very good story, Shane. Don't you know any better ones?"

"I guess I really want to apologize, Marietta, for acting the way I did. It wasn't right. I am sorry I hurt you. I didn't realize what I was doing then."

She stared at me as if I'd lost my mind.

"I deserved to pay for it, Marietta, but that clerk didn't. You didn't mean for that to happen, I'm sure."

"Like I care about a lousy clerk!"

19

I reeled back, astonished by the hatred in her eyes.

Even Keith reacted. "What's gotten into you, baby?"

"I'm not your baby." She put her hands up to her face, those long blue nails glittering in the overhead light. She pressed her hands against her cheeks, thrusting her hair back, as if trying to gain control of her thoughts.

"I hate you!" she said at last. "All of you! You just use me—us. Look at her!" She motioned toward Janice, who was out of it by now—whether drunk or stoned I didn't know. "All you care about is yourselves—all of you—Scott, Keith, Rory, Shane, even Ted. All of you. You just take what you want and you don't even think about what I want. Look at me!"

We did. She looked great in one way. But when I compared her to Alicia or Sandy's girlfriend Kathy, or even the girls in the house group, I knew she didn't have what people would call class. She was more what Sandy had once said. A tramp. And I had encouraged her to be like that.

"I'm sorry, Marietta," I said quietly.

"You—I hate you."

"I know."

She yelled suddenly, "Why are you all looking at me? Do you think this is some kind of freak show? Stop it! Stop it!"

I took a step forward, hoping to calm her down. But she interpreted it as a challenge, I guess, because she threw herself at me, hitting my chest and crying and yelling all at the same time.

My immediate instinct was to grapple with her, to get hold of her hands and push her away. Instead, I found myself putting my arms around her and just holding her against me. After a minute she stopped trying to hit me and started to cry.

"I didn't mean—oh, I don't know what I'm saying. I didn't mean for anyone to get hurt! I thought Ted could get some money and you'd be in trouble and I never meant for anything more. I just wanted you to know how it felt to be—to be so—"

"Helpless?" I said.

"I don't want to be who I am! I don't like who I am! But you and Keith and Rory—that's what you want. I don't know how to change."

I shut my eyes. For a long moment we just stood there, me holding her while she sobbed against my chest.

After a while, I opened my eyes. Sandy was still leaning against the door, but I'm sure I saw tears in his eyes before he moved to open the door and go out to get Todd and Alicia. Scott and Janice were sitting, her still on his knee, her head on his shoulder and a faraway look in her eyes.

Scott met my eyes and looked away. Keith was standing over by the wall, a few feet from us. There was a strange look on his face. "Women," he said. "They're all screwy."

Todd and Alicia came in, followed by Andrew and Ernie. Alicia helped me get Marietta onto a chair. Then Todd suggested I call Officer Martel. I had put the paper with her number in my shirt pocket. Fortunately, her apartment was fairly close. She said she'd be over in ten minutes.

While we waited, some of the other kids from the party came into the kitchen, and when they heard what had happened and that there was a cop on the way, they decided to leave. By the time Officer Martel arrived, only Scott and Janice were still around. Even Keith had disappeared.

All the anger seemed to have drained from Marietta, and with Officer Martel's encouragement, she tearfully told what had happened—how she had found my jacket that night and taken it home with her; how she had run into Ted downtown one day and he had looked pretty bad. She had taken him to a restaurant and worked out a plan for him to rob a convenience store and frame me. She found him a ski mask, and he was supposed to just threaten the clerk, not hurt him.

Except the clerk had come after Ted, and Ted had panicked and hit him with a can of juice. Had hit him hard enough that he was still in a coma.

When Marietta stopped talking, Officer Martel stood and looked around. "Whose house is this?"

We pointed to Scott.

"Where are your parents?"

He shrugged. "None of your business."

"Is she drunk or on drugs?" Officer Martel motioned toward Janice.

"She's just tired," Scott said belligerently. "If you'd all get out of my house, she could get some sleep."

Officer Martel went over and looked at Janice. "She looks about sixteen. Am I right?"

"Yes," Sandy said.

"I think your parties are over," Officer Martel said to Scott.

I guess it hadn't sunk into Scott's brain that this attractive young woman in jeans and a denim jacket was a cop.

"Who do you think you are telling me what to do?" he said.

Officer Martel was maybe five-eight, but with Scott sitting down, she was taller, and her voice was like a whip. "Get up!"

Janice giggled.

"Now!" she repeated.

Scott dumped Janice to the floor as he got up. "Now look, lady, I don't know who you think you are—"

I thought I should help him out, so I said, "She's a cop, Scott."

He sat back down.

Janice was crying. "I hurt myself!" she said angrily to Scott. "Why did you make me fall?"

"Shut up!" Scott said.

I had been holding my temper in check all night. That was too much. I took three steps to where Scott was sitting, grabbed him by the front of his shirt, and pulled him up.

"No, you shut up!" I said. "You don't just dump a girl on the floor and when she tells you she's hurt, tell her to shut up! Why did I ever start hanging around with you jerks!"

I pulled Janice to her feet.

"You're going home now, and if your dad has any sense, he won't let you out again till you're thirty! And where's your mother, anyway?"

"At home," she cried, "looking after the kids."

"Well, Sandy and Ernie are going to take you there," I looked at Officer Martel. "If that's okay with you."

"Fine. As long as you know her name and address."

I handed her to Sandy, who looked stunned.

"I'd like Alicia to come, too," he said after a moment.

I nodded.

"What about her?" I looked at Marietta.

"She'll have to go to the station. I'm off-duty. I should call and have a squad car come by."

"I'll go with her," I said.

Keith didn't say a word.

Officer Martel got on the phone and soon a couple of police cars were there. They took down everybody's names and confiscated the drugs they found. Then they took Marietta in for questioning. Todd and I followed. Everybody else went home.

Marietta's parents had been called to come down to the station, and they were not very happy. Especially her dad. He was a big man with a reddish face. Her mother looked a lot like Marietta only older and sort of faded in spite of her make-up. They looked like they'd been at a party or something. Maybe at one of the bars they owned.

I was standing beside Marietta when they came in and I saw her kind of cringe. I put my arm around her shoulders and I could feel her shaking.

"Are you okay?" I whispered.

"Yes," she said. I knew she was lying.

"Marietta, I really am sorry about everything. I want you to believe that."

"I'm sorry, too."

"What you said back at the house. About wanting to change and not knowing how. That's exactly how I felt. Only I found out there is a way. God is real, Marietta! And he gives us a second chance."

She gave me a wan smile and started to say something, but her dad came over. He'd been signing some papers so she could go home.

"Come on!" he said impatiently. Then he looked at me. "This is all your fault, you know!"

"Is it?" I asked.

He looked at me, his eyes hard. Then he grabbed her arm and pulled her out of the room. Her mother trailed behind them.

Todd came and put his arm around my shoulder.

"We'll pray for her," he said. "For all of them."

"Yeah." Who knew what would happen if we kept on praying? Marietta and Scott and Keith were no different from me. They could change, too. If we prayed enough. And if they wanted to.

We said good-night to Officer Martel and then Todd drove me home. It was about two-thirty in the morning.

Mom and Dad were sleeping, but Sandy was waiting in the kitchen. He had boiling water ready to make instant hot chocolate, which tasted pretty good.

I told him what had happened at the station and he told me about getting Janice home. She had passed out, so they had to carry her in. It was a good thing Alicia was there. Janice's mother had gone into hysterics and her father had wanted to call the cops. They had given him Officer Martel's number so he could find out for himself what his daughter had been up to.

When we had finished the hot chocolate, we went upstairs and got ready for bed.

"So—it worked," Sandy said at last.

"Yeah."

"You were lucky."

"I guess." We both knew a lot more than luck was involved.

"I'm beat." He flopped onto his bed and moments later was dead to the world.

I covered him with a blanket.

I didn't go to sleep right away. I lay on my back feeling about a dozen mixed emotions: happiness for the way things had worked out for me; concern about Marietta and Janice and the others; questions about where Ted was and what would happen now that he was wanted by the police; fear that Dad would never let Mom and me to go to the worship service on Sunday; pleasure at the way things worked out with my running and my English class; amazement at how people I didn't even know a few months ago had become so important to my life; and, most of all, hope that somehow God really would work everything out for the best.

I looked over to where Sandy was sleeping on his back, his mouth open, vulnerable for a change. It was good to know he no longer hated me.

But even better was the fact that I no longer hated myself.

20

Fortunately, the clerk Ted had beaten up did recover. It could have been a lot worse.

Marietta got a suspended sentence because she'd never been in trouble before and she didn't actually take part in the robbery. Her parents sent her to stay with an aunt, and they won't give anyone the address. I was able to get her a Bible before she left, but all I can do now is pray for her—which I am doing. So are the members of my house group and Todd and Alicia and Mr. Hwang. Oh, yeah, and Officer Martel, too.

Ted hasn't been found yet. I know Ted didn't mean to hurt anyone. He was scared and acted without thinking. I know how that feels. We're praying for him, too.

Janice doesn't talk to me or Sandy, but I hope what happened smartened her up. It's hard to say. Actually, I feel sorry for her. She can't be very happy at home.

At least she can't go to Scott's any more. His parents were speechless when the cops told them what was going on at their house. And Scott's on probation.

Keith is still Keith. He's got a new girl friend. And I think he's found another place to party.

Todd and Alicia are getting married in May. Ernie and I are both going to be ushers. That means I'll have to wear a suit. Oh, well, I guess it's for a good cause.

My life has settled into a pattern. I'm passing all my subjects. My marks are nowhere near Sandy's, but I'm happy if I just pass. Mr. McNeely wants me to go to some college where I can study writing. I don't know.

We have our first track meet this Friday. Mr. Anderson has high hopes.

I just hope I don't let him down too much.

Sandy and I have settled into a new relationship. We have our own friends, and we don't overstep the boundaries, but we talk to each other every night, and we do some things together, even if it's just playing a game on the computer.

He still thinks I'm strange because of the God bit. I'm being careful not to preach at him. The important thing is he can see the difference God has made in my life, so maybe, someday....

I found a weird verse in my Bible. It's in Proverbs 17:17. My version says, "A friend loves you all the time, and a brother helps in time of trouble." Kind of neat, huh? And it's been true for me. Ernie was my friend no matter what; and when I really needed help, even though Sandy didn't like me much at the time, he was still there for me.

My mom has changed. She's a lot happier than I remember her ever being before. She's been going to a women's house group that meets in the afternoons. And the other day she told Dad that she and I are going to start going to the worship service on Sunday. He didn't say much. Just glared at her.

He never says much to me. But he must be able to see the difference God has made. I think he's too stubborn to admit it. Mom and I are praying for him.

I feel like I should do something about Ted. No one's heard from him, and the cops have no leads. Even though I really don't know where to begin to look, I feel like I should try to find him. He needs to know that God could help him. Maybe during spring break, I'll go downtown for a few days.

That's if Mr. Golachi will give me time off. Ernie decided if I was going to have to bum money off him all the time, I should help him earn it. Just kidding. Actually, he talked Mr. Golachi into hiring me to deliver pizza for ten hours a week. Enough time to make money to pay the insurance on my car, keep it running, and buy a few snacks, but not enough to interfere with my school work. Oh, yeah, I did pay for that racquet I broke.

Life is pretty good. But Todd says not to get too comfortable. Apparently, Christians grow best when we're tested and stretched. So—I wonder what area I need to grow in next?

Best of Friends

by N. J. Lindquist

Glen Sauten:

He thinks his parents baby him a bit too much, but generally life is pretty happy for Glen, although uneventful. Until he meets...

Charlie Thornton:

The new kid in town. Charlie has everything money can buy, including a shiny, red Mustang. Furthermore, his sophistication, athletic ability, and drop dead good looks seem to attract every girl in school except...

Nicole Grant:

The pastor's daughter. Nicole is as beautiful as she is intelligent and remains unmoved by Charlie's advances—much to his frustration. And the amusement of...

Phil Trent:

Glen's best friend since kindergarten. But he is not amused to see Charlie take his place as Glen's new best friend, football quarterback, and the number one choice of every girl in town except Nicole.

Being Charlie's friend is not always easy for Glen. And keeping harmony between Charlie and Glen's other best friend, Phil Trent, is next to impossible. But it does lead to adventures. Countless adventures. In fact, Glen's whole life seems rocked by new experiences. Some of them life-threatening. And some life changing!

Friends Like These

by N. J. Lindquist

Glen Sauten:
He's just seen his life go from happily boring to roller-coaster crazy to better than his widest dreams. But it's about to go back on the roller-coaster because of...

Nicole Grant:
She seemed happy with Glen at first, but now he gets the feeling she'd like him to change. Is she confused, too, or has she made a mistake? Does she really like...

Charlie Thornton:
Having Charlie for a friend nearly got Glen killed. Dating the girl Charlie wants borders on suicidal. And Glen isn't getting much help from...

Phil Trent:
Glen's long-time best friend seems to be making matters worse, not better. But then he's got his own reasons for disliking both Charlie and Nicole.

Life hasn't become any easier for Glen. It may even have become harder. At times, he thinks he would like to go back to the old uneventful days. But you can't go back. You have to go forward. Even when you haven't a clue where you're going.

Coming soon:
> *Friends in Need*
> *More Than Friends*

If you have trouble getting our books through your local bookstore, you can order from:

That's Life! Communications

Box 487, Markham, ON L3P 3R1

Call tollfree 1-877-THATSLI(FE)
(In Toronto area (905) 471-1447)

email: thats-life@home.com

http://members.home.net/thats-life

please print

Quantity		Total
____ **In Time of Trouble** $6.95 US ($9.95 Canadian)		_____
____ **Best of Friends** $6.95 US ($9.95 Canadian)		_____
____ **Friends Like These** $6.95 US ($9.95 Canadian)		_____
____ Put me on your **mailing list** for new releases		

Name: _____

Address: _____
          apt.   street

_____
  town   prov./state   code/zip

email: _____

Shipping & handling	In Canada, GST (7%)	_____
1 book $3.00	Shipping costs	_____
2-6 books $6.00		
7-10 books $9.00	Total	_____
11+ books 10% of total		

Nancy J. Lindquist, BA, Cert. Ed. is a former English medalist, high school teacher (including Teacher of the Year), and youth worker who home-schooled her four sons until each went to high school.

Nancy's current books for teens include two non-fiction books—***The Bridge, Volumes I and II***, and two other novels—***Best of Friends*** and ***Friends Like These***. She also has an adult mystery, ***Shaded Light***.